ONE NIGHT OF *Trouble*

an After Hours novel

an After Hours novel

Elle Kennedy

This book is a work of fiction. Names, characters, places, and incidents are the product of the author's imagination or are used fictitiously. Any resemblance to actual events, locales, or persons, living or dead, is coincidental.

Copyright © 2015 by Elle Kennedy. All rights reserved, including the right to reproduce, distribute, or transmit in any form or by any means. For information regarding subsidiary rights, please contact the Publisher.

Entangled Publishing, LLC
2614 South Timberline Road
Suite 105, PMB 159
Fort Collins, CO 80525
rights@entangledpublishing.com

Edited by Gwen Hayes
Cover design by Bree Archer
Cover photography by miljko/GettyImages

Manufactured in the United States of America

First Edition January 2015

*This one is for Angie.
Ang, you're an acquired taste…but I couldn't live without you!*

Chapter One

"Hey, hot stuff, what do you say you meet me out front after you get off?" the busty blonde cooed as she sauntered up to the bar. "And then we can get *each other* off..."

AJ Walsh was torn between groaning and laughing. He found himself on the receiving end of some seriously shameless pick-up lines on a nightly basis, but this one was more blatantly sexual than most, accompanied by the seductive batting of mascara-thick eyelashes and a lewd display of lip-licking.

"Sorry, sweetheart. I'm flattered, but I've got a girlfriend," he told his would-be pursuer.

"So?" She didn't even blink.

He raised a brow. "So I'm not on the market."

The blonde wrinkled her nose in distaste. "Loser."

She took her teased hair, skintight dress, and four-inch heels, and sashayed away from the counter without ordering a thing.

The second she was gone, AJ released the laughter bubbling in his throat. Well. That was new. Being called a loser for not wanting to cheat on his girlfriend with a clearly drunk chick at a nightclub? If that made him a loser, then he didn't want to be a winner.

On the other hand, he was a *liar*, because he definitely didn't have a girlfriend at the moment. Nope, he was flying solo and hating it, but after three years of tending bar, he'd learned that sometimes a little white lie was the best way to get the more persistent women off his back.

He glanced at the other two bartenders, pleased to see them hard at work slinging drinks and chatting with the customers. Henry and Sue were his most reliable employees, and he made a point to always schedule them on Friday, the club's busiest night. Technically he didn't even need to be there tonight—his people had everything covered—but he enjoyed making drinks and getting to know his clientele.

When he'd first opened Sin with his two best friends, it had been a no-brainer as to who would handle what. Gage, the toughest and most intense of the three, was in charge of security and oversaw their team of bouncers. Reed, the most antisocial, worked in the upstairs office area and dealt with the business end of things. And as the "people person" of the trio, AJ tended bar and managed the servers.

The arrangement suited him just fine, and since their grand opening three years ago, Sin had quickly become one of the most popular clubs in downtown Boston. It had even turned a profit in its first year of business, which AJ was pretty damn proud of.

The only downside to his job was the onslaught of graphic come-ons from women he had no interest in, a turnoff that was kinda ironic considering he was a thirty-year-old, red-blooded male with a healthy libido. Other men would kill to trade places with him, AJ was fully aware of that, but he wasn't about to take advantage of the usually intoxicated females who threw themselves at him. It didn't feel right.

He'd never indulged in a one-night stand, but if he ever did, he wanted it to be with a woman who was coherent enough to know what she was doing.

As a dark head entered his line of vision, AJ voiced his standard question without even glancing at the customer. "What can I get you?"

No answer.

In the beat of silence, he focused on the woman in front of him, and his breath hitched when he got lost in a pair of bottomless brown-bordering-on-black eyes. He shifted his gaze, soaking in her delicate features, full red lips, and shoulder-length raven hair before doing a sweep of her petite body, clad in all black.

Her tank top left her arms bare, which meant he didn't miss her tattoos—a painstakingly detailed angel on her left forearm, a cluster of stars on her right biceps, and a ring of roses around her left wrist. The tats were surprisingly feminine and insanely sexy, and he suddenly had the craziest urge to strip her naked and find out if she had more ink beneath her tight top and skinny jeans.

Man. It'd been a long time since he'd experienced total lust overload. He encountered attractive women all the frickin' time, but this tiny pixie of a woman was more than attractive. The sexy combo of fragility and badassness hardened his cock, and he shifted his position so that the counter hid his lower body better.

When he realized she still hadn't spoken, he raised his voice over the pounding dance beat reverberating through the main floor. "What'll it be?"

She snapped out of whatever trance she'd fallen into, but still looked startled. A tad wary, too, but he had to be imagining it.

"Three margaritas and a Coke," she replied after another long pause.

"Coming right up." It was difficult to tear his gaze off her, but he forced himself to act professional, sliding to the other end of the counter to prepare her drinks.

He jiggled the stainless-steel margarita shaker more vigorously than necessary, a sense of nervous energy overtaking him. Fuck. He wanted to talk to her. Find out her name.

Convince her to go home with him.

And wasn't *that* a mind-boggler. He spent most nights turning down offers for sex, and all of a sudden he was imagining screwing a complete stranger?

His friends would die of shock if they could read his thoughts right now. Gage and Reed viewed him as Mr. Nice Guy, the man who held doors open for his dates and didn't sleep with a girl until they'd been seeing each other for a proper amount of time. The guy who offered women his shoulder to cry on and bought them flowers for every damn occasion.

But he supposed they had every right to see him as the nicest guy on the planet. It was the image he tried to project most of the time, the label he'd been striving his entire life to live up to.

Christ, if people only knew. How hard he worked to be that polite, dependable guy everyone could rely on. How badly he fought to suppress the wild urges that arose more often than not. How frustrating it was to dutifully play the part of prodigal son, good friend, reliable boyfriend.

He didn't always succeed, though. Sometimes the need to truly let go couldn't be ignored. He *had* to ease it, and in the past, he'd used fighting to do that. He'd heard that people frequently used sex or violence as an outlet for release, as a way to feel *alive*, and he couldn't deny that his days as an MMA fighter had certainly soothed the darker, restless part of himself that he usually hid from the world. Sex, on the other hand, didn't achieve the same result. It had always been more intimate for him, tangled up with love and relationships and all that emotional stuff.

But for some strange reason, the raven-haired woman at the counter had unleashed his carnal, reckless urges. Because suddenly the idea of going home with a stranger had become very, very appealing…

"You gonna take those over to the customer? Or just keep staring at them?"

His head jerked at Sue's teasing voice. Ignoring his aching cock, he glanced down, realizing that the drinks he'd poured were now sitting on the bar top waiting to be delivered.

"Naah, I've got it. Just spaced out for a second." He plastered on a smile, then carried the drinks over to where the woman was waiting—and staring. Staring hard, in fact, and her plump lips were puckered in the tiniest of frowns.

Unease washed over him, but he tried to ignore it. "Three margaritas and one Coke," he announced.

She gave a polite smile in return. Very, very polite…so polite it was clearly forced, and his wariness only heightened.

"Thanks," she said tightly. "How much do I owe you?"

"Eighteen bucks."

His gaze stayed on her as she dug around in her purse for her wallet. Her body language was as stiff as her voice, a clear indication that she was ticked off about something.

"Here. Keep the change." She dropped a twenty on the counter, then lifted her head and noticed him staring. "What?" she said irritably.

"You okay there? You look kinda pissed." His eyes narrowed as a thought occurred to him. "Is anyone giving you a hard time? The crowd's a little wilder than usual tonight—say the word and I'll sic one of my bouncers on whoever's bugging you."

His concern didn't spark warmth or gratitude, but more

hostility. "I'm just peachy, pal. And FYI—if someone was harassing me, I'd take care of it myself."

He studied her slim, no taller than five-two frame, his lips twitching in amusement. "Uh-huh. I'm sure you would, angel."

"I might look small, but trust me, I can kick some serious ass," she retorted.

She picked up two of the margaritas and took an abrupt step away.

AJ spoke before she could hurry off. "Is it something I said?"

A cloud of annoyance continued to hover over her. "Nope. Thanks for the drinks. I'll be back in a sec to grab these two. Make sure no one messes with them, okay?"

This time she almost made it three steps before he stopped her. And this time he didn't do it with words, but by rounding the counter, then leaving it entirely to come to her side.

Her mouth partially opened as she tilted her head to gaze up at him. "What are you doing?"

Rather than answer, he gave a quick shout in the direction of the counter. "Yo! Henry, I'm taking a break." He picked up the two glasses that remained on the counter.

"Seriously, what are you doing?" she demanded.

"Carrying these drinks back to your table. And…"

The swell of music must have drowned out his words, because she leaned in closer. "What?" she yelled.

A rush of dizziness hit him as her intoxicating scent filled his nostrils. Lord, she smelled good. Like roses in full bloom, with a trace of lavender and a hint of something entirely feminine.

He repeated himself, his tone loud and firm. "And then I plan on figuring out what I did to piss you off."

"Oh, for Pete's sake. This isn't *Cheers*—I'm not going to have a heart-to-heart with a bartender, okay? Go back to work. I can carry my own drinks."

He ignored her aggravated response. "Where are you sitting?"

She sighed with visible unhappiness, but he wasn't about to back down. His original intentions of flirting with her had temporarily been sidelined. Right now he was more interested in finding out what he'd done to put that frown on her sexy mouth. He had no doubt that this was wholly personal—the way she was scowling at him made it clear she was pissed off at *him*.

Without a word, she set off in the other direction, threading through the crowd that packed the club like sardines. AJ stayed hot on her heels, inhaling her delicious fragrance with each breath. How was it that in a room permeated with perfume, cologne, and sweat, he only seemed to be breathing in *her*?

They reached one of the tall tables spanning the back wall, and once they'd set the drinks down, his frowning pixie quickly raised the Coke to her lips, sucking hard on the straw while avoiding his eyes.

AJ watched her drink the soda, thoughtful. "So you're the Coke of the bunch. Wasn't expecting that."

She drained half the glass before answering in a terse voice. "I'm the DD." Then, ignoring him completely, she turned to the dance floor and waved at someone he couldn't see. She gestured to the margaritas, then made a cigarette-smoking motion with her hand and pointed to the side exit.

AJ glimpsed a slender blonde emerging from the dance floor to tend to the drinks, but the second he'd turned his head, the woman at his side tried to make her escape.

"Thanks for bringing the drinks. Have a good night." Her words came out in a rush.

She darted away, but AJ was equally fast, trailing after her with ease. "Where are you running off to?"

"I need some fresh air. It's hot in here."

Okay, he was totally treading into stalker territory, yet he couldn't stop himself from following her toward the exit and right out the door.

Silence greeted them in the alley between Sin and the adjacent building, broken by the occasional car honk or tire squeal from the main road beyond them. The cool spring breeze brushed over his bare arms, but he didn't mind the chill. He was too focused on his pixie's irritated face, which shone beneath the light fixture over the door.

"You're still here," she said flatly.

"Yup." He cocked his head. "And you're just telling lies all over the place, huh?"

Those mesmerizing dark eyes narrowed. "What the hell does that mean?"

"You just mimed to your friend that you're coming out for a smoke." He shrugged. "But you're not lighting up. And you told me I didn't do anything to piss you off, but obviously I did. So…" Another shrug. "Lies."

There was a pause.

And then she exploded.

"I *pretended* I was going for a cigarette so I wouldn't have to explain to my friend that I was actually trying to get away from this nosy bartender who won't leave me alone! Dude, why are you even out here? Do you harass every chick who orders a drink from you? Maybe I should be siccing one of your bouncers on *you*."

He sighed. "Tell me what I did to upset you, angel, and then I'll go."

"Would you stop calling me that?" she grumbled.

"What—*angel*? Why would I do that when it suits you oh so well?"

He brought his hand close to the tattoo on her forearm, his fingers lingering in the air. He hadn't planned on touching her, but those dark eyes that fascinated him so damn much went heavy-lidded, and then she tentatively leaned into his outstretched fingertips.

As he gently skimmed the tattoo, she let out a shaky exhale, and AJ's groin promptly stirred again. He traced the outstretched wings of the ethereal figure inked on her skin, then followed the angel's wispy dress to the tangle of vines at her feet.

Lord, her skin was hot to the touch. Silky smooth. And he didn't miss the throbbing of her pulse at the base of her slender throat, or the way her small breasts rose as she drew a deep breath.

Oh yeah. She liked having his hand on her skin. Just as much as he liked putting it there.

AJ shifted his feet again, praying her gaze wouldn't drop south. The bulge straining against his zipper was impossible to hide. His pants suddenly felt too frickin' tight, and his primal reaction to this woman made his head spin. He was usually more controlled than this, but damn it, there was no controlling the erection trying to poke right through his pants.

Or the relentless need to kiss the living daylights out of her.

"Do you really not remember me?" she blurted out.

He froze. "Do we know each other?"

Chapter Two

Ugh. Why were men so clueless?

Brett Conlon stared into the vivid green eyes of the golden boy of Hawthorne High, wondering why she'd bothered telling him the truth. She should have just pretended she didn't know who he was. At least then she'd be spared the embarrassment of him not recognizing her.

Granted, there was no reason for the star of her high school football team, Mr. Popularity personified, to remember the artsy, hell-raising girl who'd been three years behind him in school. And even though she'd hung out with an older crowd, she and AJ Walsh definitely hadn't traveled in the same circles. He'd been friends with the we're-God's-gift-to-the-world kids who made up the school's popular group, which included the snobby cheerleaders. A.k.a. the awful girls who had no qualms about harassing girls like Brett.

When she'd walked up to the bar earlier and seen AJ, all the nasty comments she'd endured back then had buzzed in her mind and instantly triggered her hostility. She'd probably been ruder than she should have, considering AJ had never ganged up on her the way his cheerleader friends had. But he'd still been present for it, and when she'd spotted him behind that counter, her hands had involuntarily circled into fists as long-ago anger and embarrassment crept in like a puddle of oozing tar.

"C'mon, you're not allowed to drop a bomb like that and not follow through," he said quietly, intently studying her face as if trying to place her.

Brett met his gaze head on. "We went to high school together."

A crease dug into his forehead. "No way. I would totally remember you if we did."

"Why? Because of the tats?" She gestured to her ink. "I didn't have these back then."

"Not the tats." Heat darkened his expression. "Your eyes. They're so dark they're almost black. I'd never forget eyes as sexy as yours."

Oh God, he was flirting with her.

AJ Walsh was flirting with her.

She suddenly had the most ridiculous urge to sprint to the ladies' room and make sure she looked okay. That her hair wasn't tangled and her mascara hadn't run. It was sad, really, how one blast from the past could turn a person into a stammering, insecure teenager all over again.

Or how one flirty remark from a guy who'd never given her a second glance in high school had caused the teenage girl inside her to do wild, excited cartwheels like the cheerleaders AJ used to hang out with.

Fortunately, the older Brett stepped in and kicked teenage Brett in the shin before she could make a total fool of herself.

"Yeah, well, my eyes haven't changed, and trust me, we went to the same school. AJ," she added meaningfully.

"The same grade?" he challenged.

She almost lied, just to make him feel bad about not

knowing who she was, but she wasn't that much of a jackass. "I was three years behind you," she admitted.

Triumph lit his expression. "Ha. See? I definitely would've remembered you if you were in my class." He shrugged. "I didn't really chill with anyone younger than me."

"Too cool for us young'uns, huh?"

"Pretty much, yeah."

The teasing smile he shot her made her heart skip a beat, and when he took a teeny step closer, she was floored by the sheer size of him. Whoa. He was a lot bigger than she remembered. He'd always been tall, but now he was *ripped*.

As his broad, muscular frame towered over her, she couldn't help but gape at his arms. Sleek, powerful biceps poured from the sleeves of his snug black tee, and his chest was so deliciously defined she could see the individual ridges of muscle rippling beneath the fabric of his shirt.

She was momentarily dazed, incapable of doing anything but full-on ogling.

Crap. It was impossible to dwell on the bad memories when he was smiling at her like that, especially when AJ's only crime in high school was being too damn popular for his own good.

"So do I ever get to learn your name, or are you withholding it as my punishment for not knowing who you were?" he asked, that boyish grin widening.

"I'm Brett."

"Brett…not usually a girl's name."

She sighed. "My mom was obsessed with Hemingway. She named me after a female character from one of his books."

"*The Sun Also Rises*," he said with a nod. "I love that book."

It didn't surprise her that he knew exactly which book she'd been talking about. Another thing she remembered about the guy—he wasn't your typical dumb jock. Nope, AJ

Walsh had been the absolute perfect package. Smart, funny, gorgeous, athletic. It was just too bad he hadn't had better taste in friends.

"So tell me," he said, sounding pensive. "What heinous crime did I commit back in the day to get you all grumpy and scowly?"

"Nothing. You did nothing." She paused. "Some of your friends weren't so nice to me, though."

"Ah. Let me guess—the cheerleaders."

A wry smile lifted her lips. "Bingo."

"Who tortured you? Tamara? Edie? They were usually the ringleaders for any nastiness that went around."

"Double bingo. Those two made my life miserable for a while."

"I'm sorry to hear that."

He sounded so genuine that she felt a pang of guilt for being rude to him before.

"If I'm being honest, I didn't pay much attention to what the girls were up to," he admitted. "I was pretty focused on football."

"I remember." She paused. "Did you ever go pro?"

"Yes and no." Before she could question that cryptic remark, he changed the subject. "So what brings you here tonight? Did you come with friends?" He rapidly answered his own question. "Wait, of course you did. Those were a lot of margaritas you ordered."

And not a single one had been for her.

Which was seriously ironic, because Brett couldn't remember the last time she'd visited a club without the intention of getting plastered.

But that was the old Brett. The wild, up-for-anything Brett who used to climb on bar counters Coyote Ugly-style and dance the night away.

The new and improved Brett didn't get into those kinds

of shenanigans anymore, and truth be told, she was proud of herself for cleaning up her act. But with the pride came shame, which tugged on her insides as she thought of the conversation she'd had with her brother Mike last month.

When he'd flat out asked her if she was an alcoholic.

She'd honestly been able to answer no, but there was also no denying she hadn't made the best choices in the past. Yes, she knew when to cut herself off, and she was perfectly capable of going for weeks, months, and even years without a drop of alcohol. Her problem wasn't getting drunk, but the decisions she made when she *was* drunk.

Like hooking up with the worst possible men for her—ahem, *Troy*—or staying out late and missing work the next morning. Or not paying her bills on time because she'd been too busy partying to remember when stuff was due.

Now that her father and brothers were monitoring her like prison guards, she couldn't afford to make those kinds of mistakes any more. She was twenty-six years old, not a dumb kid or a reckless teenager or a self-destructive young adult. It was time to grow up. Six months ago, she'd vowed to herself and her family that she would start making smart decisions.

"It's my friend's birthday," she told AJ. "We're here to celebrate."

At the thought of Jamie, a lump of guilt rose in Brett's throat. In her attempt to conduct a bad-influence cleanse, she'd had no choice but to distance herself from some of the more destructive people in her life, and unfortunately, Jamie and the girls fell under that category.

To make matters worse, her friends definitely weren't on board with her new-and-improved lifestyle. From the moment the group had arrived at Sin, the girls had been coaxing her to get drunk with them, which was not only disappointing, but disheartening. If the roles were reversed, there was no way she'd be dangling carrots of temptation in front of her friends.

She'd support their choices without question, and it saddened her that they couldn't do the same for her.

"I think I'm taking off soon, though," she added.

"I thought you were the DD," AJ said with a frown.

The lie she'd told him brought another jolt of guilt. "Naah, not really. The girls plan on closing down the place and taking a cab home. I was going to head out around midnight. Do you know what time it is now?"

AJ pulled a cell phone from his back pocket and glanced at the screen. "Eleven fifty-eight. Looks like you're about to turn into a pumpkin. Did you drive here?"

She shook her head. "I'm calling a taxi."

"Or…" His eyes gleamed recklessly.

Brett's throat went dry. "Or?"

"Or I could drive you home."

Uh-oh.

Big uh-oh.

The awareness that had sizzled between them earlier returned in full force, leaving pinpricks of heat along her bare arms. The air was cool and she'd left her coat inside, but she wasn't cold. Not by a long shot.

She knew *exactly* what would happen if she let AJ drive her home. She might have willpower when it came to alcohol, but around this man? With his sandy-blond hair and chiseled features and sparkling green eyes? And that incredible body? And throw in the fact that she hadn't had sex in six months?

Willpower? Fat chance.

"What do you say, Brett? Do you want a ride?" No missing the way his voice went husky at the word *ride*.

Oh boy. Oh boy oh boy oh boy.

This was *not* the AJ Walsh she remembered. Back then he'd come off as a gentleman.

Right now there was nothing gentlemanly about him. His expression was downright smoldering, broad body radiating pure sex appeal.

If he took her home, she knew it wouldn't end with her walking up to her apartment alone.

But she still had to make sure she wasn't misinterpreting that look on his face.

"What are you really asking me?" she said bluntly.

"I'm asking if I can take you home and screw your brains out."

Her thighs clenched so hard she almost keeled over. Okay, well, that certainly left nothing to interpretation.

"Judging by your response, I think you like the sound of that." There was something smugly *male* in his voice.

Hers was embarrassingly squeaky and as weak as her attempted ignorance. "What response?"

He flashed a knowing smile. "What, you think I can't tell when a woman is attracted to me?"

Nope, this was *not* the AJ she remembered. The golden boy was gone, replaced by a primal creature teeming with raw sexual energy. The electricity in the air was liable to burn her alive.

"Y-you…" She swallowed hard. "You don't seem like the kind of man who does stuff like this. Sleeping with someone you've just met…"

"Why do women always take it upon themselves to decide what kind of man I am?"

"Am I wrong?" she challenged.

After a beat, he gave a sheepish grin. "Fine. I haven't had a lot of one-night stands. But…" His eyes burned. "I have a feeling not going home with you tonight would be the biggest mistake of my life."

She didn't have time to absorb that intense answer, because suddenly he was touching her.

Holy hell. The air damn near incinerated when his callused fingertips stroked her wrist, sweeping over the roses inked on her skin.

"Let me take you home, Brett," he said roughly. "Let me show you who I am."

Her breath got stuck in her lungs when he brought his other hand into play. He traced the line of her jaw before sliding his palm behind her neck, then dragging it higher so he could thread his fingers through her hair.

His touch was magic. Sweet and gentle and—or not, she amended when he gave her hair a sharp tug. He nudged her head to the side to bare her throat, his spicy, masculine scent drugging her senses as his head dipped and he planted a hot kiss on her even hotter flesh.

Brett gasped at the sharp sting of teeth nipping her neck. "I know who you are," she stammered. "Or at least I thought I did."

A dark laugh fanned over her skin. "I'm pretty sure you thought wrong." He planted an openmouthed kiss right beneath her ear.

She moaned.

"Christ, you smell so fucking good." AJ rubbed his cheek on the side of her throat, his stubble scratching her hypersensitized skin.

He still hadn't kissed her on the mouth, and her lips were trembling in anticipation. When he released her and took a step back, she actually whimpered in disappointment.

"My car's parked in the back," he said huskily. "Why don't you say good-bye to your friends and then meet me in the parking lot?"

God, she should say no.

But what came out was, "Don't you have to go back to work?"

He smiled. "I'm co-owner of this place. I can take off whenever I want."

The revelation that he owned the club barely registered.

She was too focused on the curve of his lips, too entranced by the seductive smile that once again brought an ache to her core.

"Final answer?" he drawled after her silence had dragged on too long.

Say no.

Are you crazy? Say yes!

Her brain and her libido were fighting a battle inside her, and she struggled to reconcile the conflicting pleas. She really should say no. She was supposed to be making smart decisions these days—a one-night stand with a guy she knew from high school was not a smart decision. It was a reckless one.

But…damn it, he was so gorgeous she couldn't look away. And her body still tingled from his skillful touch, his hot mouth on her neck, his intoxicating scent.

She took a breath. "Yes."

He tipped his head. "Yes?"

"Yes, I'd like you to take me home."

There. She'd said it. No turning back now.

She would walk the smart-decision path tomorrow. Tonight, she was taking a detour.

She was choosing reckless.

Chapter Three

The car ride was riddled with fits and spurts of conversation, which only highlighted the problem with spur-of-the-moment decisions—they rarely ever *stayed* spur of the moment, at least not unless the invitation for sex was immediately followed by said sex. But since there'd be no sexing until they reached Brett's apartment, she had no choice but to make small talk with the man whose bones she desperately wanted to jump.

"Turn left at the next light," she told AJ, who sat behind the wheel of his black Jeep.

The slight crease in his forehead revealed that he was sensing her nervousness, and he was right to sense it. At the moment, her palms were clammy and her heart was pounding so hard it was all she could hear.

It wasn't a matter of not being attracted to him. Because she was. So badly her panties were soaked. But…this was *AJ Walsh*. All the girls in high school had fantasized about the guy, doodling his name in their binders, praying he'd say hi to them in the hall. Brett might have been an outcast, but she hadn't been immune to AJ's charms. She'd fantasized about him just as hard as everyone else, and a part of her couldn't believe those old girlhood fantasies were about to become reality.

"You okay?"

His deep voice penetrated her thoughts. Blushing, she glanced over and nodded. "I'm good. You?"

"I'm just fine, angel."

Angel.

God, now that he'd given her the nickname, he didn't seem inclined to stop using it, and each time the husky word rumbled out, a shiver rolled through her.

She rested both hands on her thighs, discreetly wiping her damp palms on the front of her jeans. Music poured out of the car speakers, the volume so low it was barely audible, but her brow wrinkled when she recognized the song.

"Is this the radio?" she asked.

"No, it's my iPod shuffle. Why?"

"You listen to Concrete Blonde?"

"I listen to a lot of things." He raised his eyebrows when he saw her face. "Why do you look so surprised?"

"I don't know...I guess it just doesn't seem like something you'd listen to."

"There you go again, making assumptions. So, tell me, what did you expect me to listen to?"

She thought it over for a moment. "John Mayer?"

A laugh popped out of his mouth. "Nope, can't say I'm a fan."

"Taylor Swift?" she suggested.

That got her a sheepish grin. "I'm not gonna lie. I think I have one or two of her songs on the shuffle."

Brett sighed. "Don't be too hard on yourself. We all have our guilty pleasures. Mine is Miley Cyrus. I blast 'Party in the USA' when I'm cleaning the house."

The song in the car faded out, then switched to the faint

sounds of hip-hop, which told her that AJ hadn't been kidding. Apparently he *did* have an eclectic taste in music.

They went quiet again, and as they got closer to her apartment, her nerves returned. AJ might have said he was okay with one-night stands, but she didn't quite believe him. No matter how dirty he'd acted back at the club, he still had good guy written all over him. His short, perfectly styled blond hair, crisp trousers and formfitting T-shirt gave him a preppy vibe—and in her experience, preppy men were usually *all* about relationships.

Well, Brett wasn't looking for a relationship. Her last one had been about as healthy as deep-fried pizza covered in chocolate, and now that Troy was no longer part of her life, she was beginning to question her habit of throwing herself headfirst into relationships. She invested so much of her heart and soul into them, to the point where she lost sight of the rest of the world.

But she didn't have time to give 100 percent to a man right now, not when too many things were up in the air at work. And if she finally convinced her father to let her run the shop, her free time would become even more limited.

"Brett?" They'd reached a stop sign, and AJ was looking at her expectantly. "Where to now?"

"Oh. Turn right. There's a shortcut on this one-way street that will take us right to my apartment."

A few minutes later, after he'd found a free parking space in front of the Korean general store she'd directed him to, he turned to her with a skeptical expression.

"You live here?"

"Yes, AJ, I live in a grocery store," she cracked. "I sleep near the deli section. Bathroom's by the frozen foods."

He flashed a sheepish smile. "I guess that was a stupid question."

"Duh." She gestured to the curtained windows above the

store. "My apartment is up there."

Her pulse sped up as they got out of the car and headed for the narrow entryway next to the dark storefront. The street was quiet and deserted, as it always was past ten o'clock. The silence was one of her favorite things about the neighborhood. Rent in Allston Village was usually pretty steep, but Brett had gotten a great deal because her landlords adored her. The Kims owned the family-run general store below her, and since she'd tattooed all six of their sons on the cheap, Mr. and Mrs. Kim had been happy to let her sublet their apartment during their extended visit to Korea. She had a one-year lease for now, but she was keeping her fingers crossed that they'd let her stay longer. The couple's eldest son, Daniel, had told her the other day that his folks were considering buying a house when they returned, which meant the apartment would be hers to keep renting.

She and AJ climbed the skinny metal steps to the second floor, where he waited patiently as she unlocked her door. She flicked on the light, then bent down to unzip her boots, while AJ looked around curiously.

He took in the mismatched furniture in the open-concept living room before shifting back to her. His seductive gaze swept over her, starting from her neon-pink socks and ending at her face.

"Want to keep making small talk?" The boyish smile he gave her was incongruous with the lust burning in his eyes.

"No." She swallowed. "I want you to kiss me."

An awkward note entered his voice. "You haven't changed your mind then?"

"I just let you into my apartment—are those the actions of a woman who's changed her mind?"

"Fair enough."

Unease washed over her. "Have you changed yours?"

"God, no." Without an ounce of hesitation, he moved

toward her, his broad body dominating her personal space.

She was painfully aware of every hard inch of him, and the dark blond stubble slashing across his strong jaw looked so tempting she couldn't help but reach up to touch it. The second her fingertips stroked his chin, a husky noise left his mouth.

"Yeah, we made enough small talk in the car," he murmured. "I think it's time we get to the fun part."

Their gazes locked. His head dipped slightly, and Brett's hand froze on his face, her lips parting with anticipation.

He rubbed her bottom lip with his thumb, making her shiver, and when he withdrew his hand, she noticed the flash of red on the pad of his callused thumb. The evidence of her bright crimson lipstick. Crap, it would probably get all over him if he kissed her. She was tempted to run to the bathroom to wipe it off, but AJ didn't give her the chance.

"You've got the sexiest lips I've ever seen," he rasped before pressing his mouth to hers.

The first kiss was gentle, just a fleeting graze and *so* not enough. Then he pulled back an inch, his breath tickling her face.

"I'm going to need a lot more than that," she complained, barely able to hear herself over the deafening hammering of her heart.

He released another husky sound, a cross between a curse and a growl, before diving in for a second taste. This time he slanted his mouth over hers in a hungry kiss. His tongue teased the seam of her lips, demanding entry, and Brett wasted no time giving him what he wanted. She moaned when their tongues met, desperately taking everything he had to offer.

Her equilibrium left her as he kissed her like a man possessed. She clutched his shoulders, holding on tight to keep from keeling over. God, the man knew how to kiss. He was greedy but controlled, firm but not forceful. And not just his mouth—his hands were equally talented. They'd moved down to her chest, cupping her breasts through her shirt and bringing little shocks of pleasure to the tips of her nipples.

She knew her breasts were small, but the way AJ groaned as he squeezed and fondled her B-cups, you'd think she had porn-star tits.

"I need to see you. Take the shirt off. Now." A command, low and sultry, inviting no argument.

She responded with a throaty challenge. "Do it for me."

Without a word, he reached for the hem of her tank top and slowly dragged the material upward. He stopped before her breasts were exposed, toying with the bottom of the shirt, callused thumbs stroking her stomach for a moment. Then he slipped the shirt up and over her head, and another noise escaped his lips. Definitely a growl this time.

"No bra?" he rumbled.

"No point," she replied silkily. "My boobs are too little. I only wear one in the winter to cover my nipples. They get really hard and pointy when I'm cold."

"They're hard right now," he taunted. "Are you cold?"

A breath shuddered out. "No."

"Are you turned on?"

"Yes."

He smiled. Didn't make a single move.

Brett fought an odd rush of self-consciousness as he focused on her puckered nipples. God. She was standing there topless—and his hands were resting at his sides. Why wasn't he touching her, damn it?

"What's that distressed look for?" he teased. "You need something from me, Brett?"

"You *know* what I need," she blurted out. "Touch me. *Please.*"

His lips curved seductively. "But I'm not done admiring

you."

"You're not done tormenting me, you mean." She glared at him. "You know, you're really not as nice as you look."

"Isn't that what I've been telling you all along?" His smile widened. "There's nothing nice about what I'm going to do to you tonight."

And then he touched her.

And he was right. It wasn't nice. It was…sheer magic. He was rougher than she'd expected, squeezing her breasts hard enough to send a jolt of pleasure right down to her core. Her thighs clenched when he pinched her nipples, unleashing an uncontrollable shiver of need.

Chuckling, AJ bent down and drew one nipple in his mouth.

Sweet baby Jesus.

The heat of his mouth and wetness of his tongue made her see stars. Someone call the press—*because AJ Walsh was sucking on her nipple*. Never in a million years would she have dreamed that the golden boy of her high school would be doing that to her. To *her*, the screwup loner who'd attracted nothing but unwanted attention at Hawthorne High.

But there was no power imbalance tonight. They were no longer teenagers from different social groups. They were a man and a woman, capable of driving each other wild, and even though AJ was currently the one worshipping *her* body, Brett had no doubt that he was as turned on as she was.

He hissed with approval as he took deep pulls on her nipples, alternating from one to the other, sucking so hard her breasts pulsed with pleasure. When he slid a hand between her legs and cupped her mound, another shockwave hit, so intense she could barely stay upright.

Whimpering, she grabbed his hair, yanked his head up, and brought their mouths together in a violent kiss. As her hands clawed at his belt, AJ's laughter tickled her lips.

"Someone's feeling eager," he murmured.

"Hell yeah."

He intercepted her hand before she could undo his belt buckle. "Hmmm. Then maybe I should make you wait."

"Why on earth would you do that?" she demanded.

"Maybe I want to hear you beg."

Brett shot him a smug look. "That's not going to happen. I don't beg."

"No?"

"Nope. I just take what I want." With that, she shoved his hand away and pulled the strip of leather free from the buckle. "And what I want right now is you. Naked. Got a problem with that?"

Chapter Four

As the impatient woman in front of him skillfully stripped him of his clothes, only one thought ran through AJ's head—*no more Mr. Nice Guy.*

Oh no, there was nothing nice about what he was doing right now. He'd brought a beautiful woman home for the sole purpose of fucking her brains out, and damned if that wasn't the most liberating sensation on the planet. He didn't have to be the good guy tonight. Didn't have to be polite or take it slow or worry about the repercussions. Brett's eagerness made it clear that she wanted this as much as he did.

Their clothing disappeared in the blink of an eye. His pants and shoes were kicked away; her jeans and panties skidded across the living room floor. Brett's smooth, naked flesh assaulted his vision, making his mouth go dry and his heartbeat race.

Just as he'd anticipated, her ink wasn't confined to her arms. Her left thigh boasted an exquisite koi fish done in brilliant greens and blues, while her right hip was covered with a row of text written in meticulous cursive. And her feet—she had two pale blue sparrows tattooed on the top of each graceful foot, and it was the hottest frickin' thing he'd ever seen in his life.

She wasn't overly curvy, but soft in all the right places, and his arousal soared to a whole new dimension as he yanked her toward him and pressed their naked flesh together. He reached down to cup her ass, giving it a light squeeze that drew a tortured noise from her lips.

Christ. There were so many things he wanted to do to her he didn't even know where to begin. As his heart pounded and his brain turned to jelly, AJ decided to just start from the top and work his way south.

Breathing hard, he nudged her to the overstuffed couch and pointed to the cushions. "Lie down."

He didn't have to ask twice—she was on her back in a nanosecond, her legs parting enticingly as she stretched out on the sofa.

AJ covered her body with his, then propped himself on his elbows and slid lower so he was at eye level with her breasts. Lord, those breasts. Small and plump, with the prettiest nipples he'd ever seen.

"You have the sweetest tits," he mumbled.

He rubbed his mouth over one distended bud, enjoying the way it tickled his lips. His cock was harder than granite, heavy against Brett's thigh and throbbing so badly he worried he might actually come if Brett's leg so much as twitched. He distracted himself from the fiery ache below by capturing one nipple between his lips. He sucked hard, his teeth grazing the rigid pink bud.

He was being much rougher than usual, and he tried to rein himself in, to be tender and sweet and *nice*, but goddamn it, he couldn't. He wanted to *devour* her.

Luckily, she didn't seem to mind. Not one bit.

"God, keep doing that," she pleaded when he shifted to

her other nipple and took a gentle bite.

He did it again, and again, until she was squirming beneath him, rocking her hips in a blatant attempt to deepen the contact. His erection brushed her slippery folds each time her eager body arched upward, and the temptation to slide into her was so strong he had no choice but to eliminate it by moving lower.

His mouth left her breasts—and discovered an even greater temptation.

"Hell," he said hoarsely. "You're perfect." He dragged a finger up and down her slit, groaning when he glimpsed the sparkle of moisture at her entrance. "So fucking pretty."

He planted a kiss directly on her clit and enjoyed the way she gasped. She spread her legs wider, granting him full access to explore, and AJ's brain stopped working altogether as he buried his face between her thighs. Given her earlier response to his rough ministrations, it didn't surprise him in the slightest that she liked the less than gentle approach more than the teasing one. She whimpered at each soft lick, but moaned like crazy when he sucked deeply on her clit. She sighed when he stroked her opening with one finger, but cried out in delight when he pushed it into her hot channel and fingered her with fervor.

Her inner muscles clamped around him, sending a bolt of anticipation straight to his cock. She was so damn tight. He couldn't wait to get inside her.

But he wanted to make her come first.

"Don't keep me waiting, angel—come on my tongue. I *need* it." Christ, he did. Needed it so bad he could barely breathe.

He swiped his tongue over her clit, slipping a second finger into her pussy as he lost himself in the taste of her, in the throaty noises she was making and the sharp sting of her fingers in his hair as she tried to hold him in place.

"I'm close," she squeezed out. "Don't stop. Please don't stop."

Ha. *Stop?* Like that was even possible. He was so turned on, so consumed with the need to feel her pulsing on his tongue, that not even the Jaws of Life could have pried him off her. And when she started to convulse, pure male satisfaction coursed through his veins. He rode out the orgasm with her, his tongue toying with her clit as it swelled and pulsated from her release.

When she grew still, AJ raised his head and wiped his mouth with the back of his hand. He took in her glazed eyes, limp body, and unstable breathing, and a smile sprang to his lips.

"Oh my God," she mumbled, her sigh of pleasure heating the air between them. "That was *so* good. I'm going to make you do that at least five more times before the night is over. I hope you know that."

He laughed. "Demanding, aren't we?"

"Dude, if I'd known you were *this* talented, I wouldn't have hesitated earlier about bringing you home. Seriously, I want to lock you in my bedroom closet and put your tongue to use whenever I'm stressed out."

With another chuckle, he planted one last kiss on her mound before rising to his feet. His cock jutted out eagerly and slapped his navel, as if to say *my turn*. But his pants—and the condom in his wallet—were all the way across the room, and he was hurting too damn bad to make the trek at the moment.

"Sit up," he said in a low voice.

She obeyed without question, her dark eyes blazing with unabashed lust as he fisted his cock and gave it a slow pump.

He'd never jerked off in front of a woman before, but the hitch in Brett's breath told him she liked seeing him do it. So he didn't stop. He tightened his grip around his shaft, moving his hand in long, hard strokes that made his balls tingle and his knees weak.

"That's the hottest thing I've ever seen," she whispered. "You're so damn sexy."

He might've been able to keep going—if she hadn't moved her hand between her legs and started stroking her clit. The sight nearly did him in. He had to grit his teeth and breathe through his nose to stop from coming, and once he was confident he could take a step without blowing his load, he moved to the couch with purposeful strides and guided his cock to her lips.

"Suck," he said.

The crude command was another first for him, but he was too worked up to worry about manners. The second Brett parted her lips, he pushed through them, groaning when the heat of her mouth surrounded him.

His head lolled to the side as pleasure sizzled through his body. Her mouth was warm and wet and hungry. She swallowed him up, eager tongue skimming his shaft on every upstroke. Then she sucked hard on the crown of his cock, and the muffled sound of contentment she made retriggered that uncontrollable urge to come.

He withdrew slightly, meeting her eyes as she peered up at him. "Go slow," he instructed. "Lick the shaft nice and slow. Suck only on the tip. And play with my balls."

More demands. Christ. Who *was* he? Yeah, he was vocal in the bedroom, but not usually to this extent.

What was different about tonight? Was it because he'd probably never see Brett again? Maybe. No, definitely. For some reason, knowing that this was only a one-night stand had eliminated his typical need to restrain and censor himself.

Another rush of liberation flooded his gut as realization struck. His mindset was eerily similar to the way he felt when he was kicking ass in the cage. He could do and say whatever he wanted tonight. He didn't have to hold back, didn't have to worry about coming on too strong. Yes, he would take care of her—he already had and planned on doing it again—but he could also be selfish. For this one night, he could drop the good-guy mask and act on the primal urges he'd been fighting his entire life.

"That's it, tease me." He shuddered when she licked the sweet spot on the underside of his cock. Gentle and seductive. "I don't want to come yet. Just get me ready."

She tightened the suction, and when his hips gave an involuntarily thrust, she reached around and cupped his ass, taking him all the way to the back of her throat. She paused for a moment.

"There you go. Breathe." AJ stroked her hair, the dark strands soft and silky between his fingers. He pulled almost his entire length out, until only the tip remained between her lips, and then he slipped inside again with the same leisurely tempo.

Christ. There was nothing better than this. A nice, lazy blowjob. Brett's tiny whimpers of pleasure. The pressure of her fingers digging into his butt cheeks.

But the impatience built, the acute need for release gathering in his balls until he had no choice but to wrench his cock out of her hot mouth.

"Where are you going?" she demanded when he took several steps away.

"Condom," he choked out.

He grabbed his pants off the floor and fumbled in the pockets for his wallet. Once he found what he was looking for, he sheathed himself in an impressive feat of speed and strode back to the couch.

Brett was lying down again, a slight smirk on her face as she looked up at him. "If you're not inside me in the next two seconds, I'm going to be very upset."

"Don't worry, there's nowhere else I want to be." To punctuate that, he lowered his body on top of hers, grasped his erection, and guided it to her core.

The first thrust had black dots flashing in his vision. Holy hell. She was just as tight as he'd anticipated.

"First time is gonna be fast," he warned her. "I'm way too close."

She smiled, her dark eyes gleaming with feminine power. "You can make it up to me later. With your tongue."

"Oh, I intend to," he growled. "With my tongue. And my hands. And my cock. By the time this night is over, you'll be so well fucked you won't be able to move for days."

He buried himself to the hilt, and this time they groaned in unison.

"I. Can't. Wait," she burst out. Each word was a moan, because he was moving inside her now, fast and deep.

The couch cushions squeaked from the frantic pace he'd set. He'd turned into an animal, driving into her without restraint, sucking and biting her neck as pleasure rippled through his body. His surroundings faded. His pulse shrieked between his ears. All he was conscious of was the woman beneath him. Her hot sheath gripping his cock. Her moans echoing in his ear.

The climax hit him like a sledgehammer to the chest. Knocked the wind right out of him as paralyzing ecstasy pulsed in the base of his spine and then shot out in every direction. He wasn't sure when—or how—he crashed back to the earth, but when he was able to think clearly again, he registered Brett's soft laughter.

"What?" he croaked.

Her wide grin pierced through his foggy vision. "Nothing. I was just thinking that if I'd known you were this good of a lay, I would've tried harder to hook up with you in high school."

He choked out a laugh of his own, gently easing out of her core before collapsing at her side. He ran his hand over her breasts, but his fingers still felt like limp noodles, so he splayed them over her flat belly and nestled closer to her. "Trust me, you didn't miss out. I was an amateur back then. No moves."

"An amateur, huh?" Her lips tickled his shoulder. "Does that make you a professional fucker now?"

"Yup." He moved his hand over her stomach in a sensual caress. "These days I know what I'm doing."

"God. You totally do." She sat up and brushed hair off her forehead, then gave him a little shove so that he was on his back. "Okay, that was a long enough break. Let's do it again."

Her eagerness made him laugh, but she silenced the husky sound with a kiss.

And proceeded to rock his world all over again.

They slept. They screwed. Slept some more. Screwed some more.

By the time AJ crashed for the night, he'd reached several important conclusions. One—casual hookups were not as sleazy as he'd previously believed. Two—it *was* possible to pass out from sex-exhaustion. And three—he'd had the best sex of his life tonight. Hands down.

Those warm and fuzzy thoughts carried him into slumber, and he wouldn't have been surprised to learn that he'd fallen asleep with a smile on his face. God knew he woke up with one.

The moment he opened his eyes the next morning and found Brett curled up beside him in bed, his lips curved in satisfaction.

They'd eventually found their way into her bedroom, and were now tangled together between the sheets. She was naked, one leg hooked over his hip, one arm flung across his chest. The beams of sunlight slipping into the room through the gap in the curtains cast a halo of light around her face, and he smiled when he saw that her cheek bore the impression of the blanket.

She really was beautiful. Not in the classic sense, but in an interesting way. Her mouth was a tad too wide, her chin a little too angular, and those dark eyes were too big for her face, yet the combination of details created a striking package that fascinated him.

He would've liked to give her a wake-up she'd never forget, but unfortunately, his bladder wasn't cooperating. Stifling a curse, he slid out of bed and quietly searched the bedroom for something to wear. His clothes had been abandoned in the living room, but he felt weird walking around naked in Brett's apartment, so he swiped the pink towel that had haphazardly been tossed on the dresser and quickly wrapped it around his waist.

It only took a minute to pop into the hall bathroom and do his business, but just as he was about to head back to the bedroom, a loud *creak* echoed through the apartment.

AJ froze.

Was that the front door?

Shit. It was.

Heavy footsteps suddenly thumped from the hall, accompanied by a deep male voice. "Brett? You up?"

Fucking hell. Did Brett have a *boyfriend*?

The thought flew into AJ's head like a fastball, bringing a jolt of panic. He hadn't thought to ask her last night, but… she *had* to be single, right? She wouldn't have slept with him if she wasn't.

Right?

He was two seconds from diving into the bedroom when the footsteps got closer. "Yo, why are there clothes on the living room floor? I thought you learned how to pick up after yourself—"

A tall, dark-haired man rounded the corner and stopped in his tracks.

"Oh. Hi." Confused dark eyes collided with AJ's sheepish face before narrowing in suspicion. "Who the hell are—*Walsh*?"

Recognition dawned on the other man's face at the precise moment that AJ experienced a déjà vu of his own. "Conlon?" he said in surprise.

"Holy shit, it *is* you." Rob Conlon broke out in a broad smile. "AJ Walsh. Dude, it's been *years*."

Many years, in fact. AJ hadn't seen Rob since high school, and Conlon was the last person he'd expected to run into this morning—while wearing a *pink* towel.

AJ studied his former classmate, noting that the guy hadn't changed much over the years. Rob was as tall as he'd been back then, with the same cropped haircut and scruffy facial hair. Definitely more muscular, though, and the full-sleeve tattoos were also new.

"How've you been, man?" Rob charged forward to pull AJ in for a macho side hug, which he uneasily returned.

"I'm good. You?"

"Doing great." As Rob took a step back, the joy he'd been emitting reverted back to distrust. His gaze lowered to the towel slung around AJ's hips, as if he'd just noticed the pink monstrosity.

"What are you doing here?" Rob asked warily. "Where's my sister?"

Sister?

Oh crap. Brett was Rob's *sister*?

But a hasty examination of the other man's face was all it took to spot the resemblance. They had the same eyes, AJ realized, though while Rob's features were sharply masculine,

Brett's were soft and delicate. Not to mention that Rob Conlon was a frickin' mountain compared to Brett's pixie frame.

"Seriously, where the hell is she?"

AJ was about to answer, but Brett's calm voice cut him off.

"I'm right here." Like a graceful feline, she sauntered out of the bedroom wearing an oversize T-shirt that hung to her knees.

AJ saw through her composed facade. She'd clearly thrown her shirt on in a hurry—the damn thing was inside out—and her hair was noticeably tousled from sleep...and other much less innocent activities. AJ remembered tangling his fingers through that inky-black hair many, many times last night. Pulling on it, too. Hard.

Before he could stop it, a parade of vivid memories marched into his head, the most prominent involving Brett's lips wrapped around his cock.

He had to will his lower body not to respond, because the last thing he needed was to spring a boner in front of Brett's *brother*. Christ. That would go over like a punch to the face.

A literal one, most likely. With AJ's face being the one in question.

"What are...?" Rob looked from AJ to his sister. "I didn't realize you two knew each other."

AJ would have given his left arm to be able to fade into his surroundings. The friendly reception he'd received from Rob had all but disappeared, and the man was currently eyeing him like he'd pickpocketed his wallet or some shit. Gone was the old friend from high school—replaced by a big brother in full-on protection mode.

"Well, we do know each other." Brett's tone was flippant, but AJ didn't miss the flush rising in her cheeks. "What are you doing here? I thought we talked about calling before you stop by."

Rob ignored her. His scowl deepened as he turned to AJ. "Why are you at my sister's apartment at nine in the morning?"

AJ had to choke back a laugh. Talk about the most obvious question on the planet. He was wearing a *pink towel*, for fuck's sake.

On the same token, there was no way in hell he was admitting to Brett's brother that he'd picked her up at the club last night and brought her home for sex.

To his relief, Brett didn't seem interested in sharing that juicy tidbit, either. "What are you doing here?" she repeated.

"Why is Walsh here?" her brother countered.

Brett's hands curled into small fists at her sides, and AJ could tell she was trying very hard not to lose her temper.

He searched his own brain for a suitable response, one that didn't feature the words *one-night stand* or *hot, sweaty sex*, but again, Brett beat him to the punch.

"He's here because he's my boyfriend."

Chapter Five

Shit on a stick.

Of all the times her big brother had showed up unannounced, this had to be the worst. She'd *finally* been making headway in her quest to prove that she'd put her wild partying days behind her. She'd even managed to finagle a promise out of Rob that he'd speak to their dad on her behalf and vouch for her new, responsible ways.

Now any endorsement from her brother was about to be shot to hell. He'd just walked in on her and her one-night stand, for Pete's sake—how was *that* going to convince him she'd changed? And no matter how tough he looked, Rob happened to be the biggest daddy's boy in her family, which meant he'd rat her out in a heartbeat.

Panic scurried up her spine as she envisioned her infuriating brother telling their dad about the scene he'd just stumbled on.

Crap. She couldn't let that happen.

Please, please, please just go with it.

She silently pleaded at AJ from behind her brother's

head, praying that he'd back her up. AJ's green eyes had filled with surprise at her announcement, and she could practically see his brain working to make sense of it.

"Your boyfriend?" Rob said incredulously. "Since when?"

AJ spoke up before Brett could. "It's been a few weeks now."

The response was so smooth and sounded so genuine that even Brett believed him, and she *knew* he was lying. A rush of gratitude flooded her belly, which she tried to convey wordlessly when their gazes locked again.

"Yeah?" Rob shook his head a few times, still looking confused. But it didn't take long for him to adjust. With a big grin, he glanced over at Brett and said, "This is awesome. Dad will be thrilled."

She furrowed her brow. "He will?"

"Are you serious? You're dating the Ten Grand Touchdown!" her brother exclaimed. "I bet he throws you a celebratory parade."

Her confusion only heightened. "What the hell are you babbling about?"

Rob sighed heavily, as if he couldn't *believe* the comment even warranted an explanation. "Remember that game back in senior year, when half the Hawks players got injured the week we were scheduled to play the division leaders?"

"No."

He kept going as if she hadn't spoken. "Nobody thought we stood a chance of winning that game—bookies were giving us twenty-to-one odds. Well, Dad bet five hundred bucks on the Hawks." Rob shook his head in amazement. "End of the fourth, we're down by six, one play left, and then this guy"—he gestured to AJ—"ends up catching a Hail Mary in the end zone."

"Oh crap, I remember that game," AJ blurted out, laughing softly. "I'm pretty sure I was as shocked as everyone else in the stadium when I actually caught that pass." He paused. "Your dad bets that kind of money on high school football games?"

"Oh yeah. He bets on everything." Rob was still grinning from ear to ear. "He worships the ground you walk on, dude. To this day, he still brags about that payout."

Brett had a vague recollection of her father boasting about some touchdown that had made him a lot of money, but as the only female in a family of males, she'd learned to tune out her dad and brothers whenever they jabbered on about sports.

And as the youngest sister of three overbearing older brothers, she was used to them interfering in her life, and so it didn't surprise her that Rob didn't make a single move to leave, despite the fact that he was certainly *not* welcome at the moment.

"Do you still talk to Miller?" Rob asked AJ. "I remember you two were tight."

"Yup. Actually, we co-own a nightclub together."

Brett wrinkled her nose. Were they talking about Reed Miller? She remembered him from high school, too. Reed had been a bad boy to the core, and not someone she'd seen AJ hanging out with.

The fact that the two men had been close, and apparently still were, made her realize she hadn't known AJ at all back then. She'd invented a fantasy version of him, one that included a load of assumptions that he'd rapidly poked holes in since the moment they'd crossed paths again.

"It's a shame he got kicked off the team. He was damn good."

"Yeah, Reed was a force of nature on that offensive line."

Much to her displeasure, the two men were oblivious to her presence now, chatting as if she weren't even in the room.

"I heard you got into MMA," Rob said.

It took a serious effort to keep her jaw closed. AJ was a mixed martial arts fighter? Since *when*?

"Yeah, I fought pro for a few years. So did Reed."

Brett opened her mouth to press for details, but her brother didn't give her the chance.

"That's hardcore." Nodding with approval, he looked over at Brett again. "Honestly, B? Normally your taste in dudes *sucks*, but I'm totally digging this arrangement."

"Wonderful. I'm glad you approve." She crossed her arms and fixed him with a glare. "Now will you please go away? I'll see you at the shop in an hour."

Rob rolled his eyes. "Fine. I'm gone. I know when I'm not wanted." He stepped forward to give AJ a hearty slap on the shoulder. "I'm sure I'll be seeing a lot more of you, man. Actually, I'll see you tomorrow, right?"

AJ blinked. "Tomorrow?"

Rob turned to Brett with visible displeasure. "You didn't invite him to the barbecue?"

She stifled a groan. Crap. Why had she lied, damn it? She'd never had a problem inviting boyfriends to family events in the past, and now that she'd launched this foolish charade, it would look insanely suspicious if she didn't bring AJ over to her dad's place tomorrow.

"Of course I invited him, but he might have to work." She stalked forward, forcibly dragging her brother away from AJ and toward the front hallway. "It's time for you to go. I have to shower and get ready for work."

"Fine. We'll talk later."

Since he was a good foot taller than her, he had to hunch over in order to plant a kiss on the top of her head, and the familiar gesture instantly had her softening. As nosy and overprotective as her brothers could be, she still adored each and every one of them and knew they felt the same way about her.

"I'll see you in a bit, okay?" she said, squeezing his arm.

The second the door closed behind him, Brett released a sigh of relief and made a beeline to the bedroom, where she found AJ getting dressed.

She lingered in the doorway for a moment, soaking in the sight of his lean, muscular body. The way his abs tightened as he pulled a shirt over his head, the flexing of his biceps as he reached down to zip up his pants. Now that Rob was gone, she allowed the memories of last night to flood her mind, and the wicked images made her heart beat faster. God, it had been an incredible night. She hadn't expected AJ to be so...*dirty*.

His head turned sharply as he became aware of her presence. Then he relaxed and offered a wry look. "So."

"So." She drew a deep breath. "I guess we should talk about the whole boyfriend thing."

To her surprise, he smiled at her. "Naah, I get it. You didn't want your brother to think we had a casual hookup. Makes sense to me."

"Normally I wouldn't care what Rob thinks, but there's some stuff happening right now, and..." A sigh slipped out. "Truthfully, my past isn't very spotless. I've done some stupid stuff I'm not particularly proud of, which includes going out with a lot of assholes. I don't sleep around," she added hastily, not wanting him to think she was a raging ho-bag or anything. "But I haven't picked many winners in the love department. And my family is already super overprotective because I'm the youngest, so my rebellious bullshit didn't exactly help the situation."

"I can imagine. I remember Rob from high school. He was very in-your-face, always thought his way was the right one." AJ's head tipped thoughtfully. "You have another brother, right? A year younger than Rob?"

She nodded. "That's Jordan. Me, Rob, and Jordan were all born a year apart. And our brother Mike is two years older than Rob. My folks wanted all their kids to be close in age. That's what both their families were like, all the siblings only a year or two apart."

Her cheeks warmed as she realized she was reciting her family history to him like she was in a genealogy seminar, but she was nervous again, and when she got nervous, she babbled.

As if sensing her agitation, AJ crossed the room and swept a gentle hand over her cheek. It amazed her how attuned he was to her every response.

That keen intuition definitely extended to sexual responses, too. Because holy moly, the man had rocked her world last night. He'd known exactly where to touch her, how to make her scream, moan, beg... Yep, she clearly remembered doing some begging, just like he'd promised her she would.

Bottom line: AJ Walsh had dominated every inch of her last night.

And she was dying for him to do it again.

He must have glimpsed the sexual longing in her expression, because heat flared in his own eyes. "That was some really good sex, huh?"

"*Amazing* sex," she corrected.

Their gazes held. A bolt of awareness streaked between them. AJ's gaze dipped to her bare legs, and the predatory gleam she witnessed sent a shiver dancing through her.

God, she wanted him again.

And if the growing bulge beneath his zipper was any indication, he wanted her too.

"Anyway." Brett cleared her throat, trying to drag her mind out of the gutter. "I'm in the process of trying to convince my family that I've cleaned up my act, and right now it's more important than ever to prove myself to them."

"Why is that?" He led her to the bed and tugged her down beside him.

"My family owns a couple of tattoo parlors. Rob runs the one in Southie—I work there as an artist—and then there's the west-side location that opened a couple years ago. Mike manages that one. But my dad is planning on opening a third location in the north end." She let out a breath. "I want to run it."

"Ah. I see. What about your other brother?"

"Jordan?" She couldn't help but laugh. "Poor guy can't even draw a straight line—seriously, he has no artistic talent whatsoever. He's a mechanic." She squared her shoulders. "And even if Jordan *was* in the business, I'd be a way better manager than him. Except…well, my track record isn't really helping my cause." Her posture drooped. "My dad thinks I can't handle the responsibility."

"What happens if you don't manage the shop? Will your father do it?"

"No, he's really keen on retiring. He'd have to hire an outsider." Frustration jammed in her throat. "But I know he'd rather keep the business in the family, and I *know* I can manage that shop. I'd be really good at it."

"Of course you would."

The conviction in his tone startled her. AJ barely knew her, yet he sounded more confident of her abilities than all her brothers combined.

"Dad gave me six months to prove I'm mature enough to run the business, and my time is almost up. He's supposed to give me an answer at the end of the month." A stab of misery twisted her stomach. "I was finally starting to convince them I'm not the party girl I used to be. That's why I told Rob we're dating. If he knew I brought a stranger home for the night, he'd totally tell my dad."

"Seriously? He'd do that?"

"Oh yeah," she said grimly. "There are no secrets in my family. And they all *hated* the last guy I was seeing. Troy was the least reliable person on the planet, and the two of us brought out the worst in each other. My family already thinks I have terrible taste in men—the last thing I need is them finding out that I had a one-night stand."

"I get it." AJ's tone grew oddly strained. "I know all about family expectations."

"You do?"

He nodded, but rather than offer any details, he suddenly flashed that boyish smile she was growing accustomed to. "All right. Ask me."

She knit her brows. "Ask you what?"

"To be your pretend boyfriend. Isn't that what this heart-to-heart has been leading to?"

Brett faltered. "Actually, I was only going to invite you to the barbecue. I figured a few days after that, I can just tell them I dumped you."

Those green eyes sparkled. "Bullshit. They'd never believe it."

"Why not?"

"Because I'm fucking awesome, Brett. You'd *never* dump me."

"Gee, it's good to know you don't suffer from any confidence deficiencies."

"Seriously, it would look too suspicious if you announce out of the blue that we broke up. Besides…" The twinkle in his eye turned to smoky promise. "We have the perfect opportunity here, and I'm not about to pass it up."

"What opportunity?" she said slowly.

"To turn this one-night stand into a several-nights stand." AJ smiled again, and a dimple she hadn't noticed before appeared in his chin. Sweet Lord, the guy was unbelievably cute.

No, he wasn't cute. He was *sexy*. And she'd be lying through her teeth if she said the idea of sleeping with him again wasn't incredibly appealing.

As if he'd read her mind, his voice grew low and husky. "You still want me as much as I want you."

"Oh, do I?" she mocked.

"Don't play games, angel. We both know it's true." He paused. "Your dad is giving you an answer at the end of the month, right?"

She nodded warily.

"That gives us three and a half weeks to keep doing what we're doing." There was no mistaking the reckless glint in his eyes.

"And what exactly *are* we doing?"

"Having fun. Making each other come."

She ignored the hot shiver that traveled up her spine. "And then what?"

"Then your dad gives you the manager job, you tell your family we broke up, and we go our separate ways."

Biting her lip, Brett mulled over what was beginning to sound like a solid plan—especially the sex part. Three more weeks of super-sexy naked time with this man? Sign her up.

But the idea held more than just sexual merit. If she said yes, then she'd be "dating" a guy that screamed wholesome and responsible, which was a surefire way to show her family she'd changed.

"It's not a bad idea," she admitted.

AJ looked smug. "Told ya."

"As long as we're both clear that this won't be a real relationship," she said quickly. "I'm not looking to get seriously involved with anyone right now, and once I have my own tattoo parlor to run, I won't have time for a relationship at all." She chewed on her lip, still deep in thought. "But I probably don't have to worry about this being anything more than a fling, right? I mean, I know where I stand, and you… well, I'm pretty sure I'm not your type, anyway…so…"

"Trust me, I don't have time for a relationship, either." His face took on a shuttered expression. "It'll be a pretend relationship."

That he didn't correct her assumption about not being his type kind of stung. It shouldn't, though. Of course he wouldn't view her as girlfriend material. She was scrawny and covered in tattoos and the furthest thing from meek. A man like AJ belonged with some sweet, docile thing who'd bake him cookies and rub his feet, not an ex-bad-girl tattoo artist with a chip on her shoulder.

"The sex, though…that won't be pretend at all." AJ's voice became downright sensual. "Because there's no way I can spend three weeks with you and *not* put my hands all over that sexy-ass body."

The saliva in her mouth turned to sawdust. "I'd kill you if you *didn't* put your hands on me."

"Threatening me with murder, huh? And last night you threatened to lock me in your closet." He arched a brow. "For such a teeny little thing, you've got some pretty violent tendencies."

"Like I said, I'm tougher than I look." She pursed her lips. "So it's official then? You'll be my pretend boyfriend?"

"Yup." He grinned. "Provided I'm well compensated."

"I already said I'd sleep with you again," she grumbled. "And you didn't even have to twist my arm."

"That's not all I want."

Brett's guard shot up, especially when she saw the intensity hardening his chiseled features. "What else, then?"

"I want you to show me a wild time."

The demand triggered a jolt of uneasiness. "I told you, I don't party anymore," she said firmly.

"I don't want to party. I just want to have some fun." Something she couldn't decipher flickered through his expression. "All I ever do is follow the rules." He shrugged.

"I'm in the mood to break some."

Hunger, she realized. It was hunger flashing in his eyes. And seeing it only heightened her reluctance. "I'm not sure I can help you with that."

His hand was on her cheek again, but not gentle this time. Rough fingertips did a seductive sweep over her skin, grazing her bottom lip. "I'm not asking you to snort coke or streak through Boston Common with me. I just want… Hell, I just want to be the man I was last night. The man I was with you."

Some of her caginess dissipated. "You mean, the man who bossed me around and gave me the best orgasms of my life?" A tiny smile broke free. "If that's all you want, then I think I can get on board with that."

With a pleased nod, he grasped her chin and brought her mouth to his.

The kiss was deep and forceful. Dominating. And just like last night, she was instantly sucked into his seductive spell, losing herself in the firmness of his lips and the greedy strokes of his tongue. Everything about this man drove her wild, from his heady masculine scent, to the scrape of his stubble on her cheek. She was addicted. Goddamn addicted.

Somehow, she managed to wrench her lips away, breathing hard as she recovered from that toe-curling kiss. "I have to get to work," she told him. "I can't be late."

AJ swiftly rose to his feet, pulling her up with him. "What time are you done?"

As he spoke, he lightly caressed her cheek again, as if he couldn't go a single second without touching her. Brett had zero complaints about that. Every time those big, warm hands connected with her skin, it felt like her entire body was engulfed by flames.

"We close at nine. But if it's dead, I'm usually out of there by eight."

"Come to the club when you're finished."

It wasn't a question. It was a command. But she wasn't complaining about *that*, either. She was discovering that his dominance was as addictive as his touch.

"Use the staff door in the back of the building," he added. "Hit the intercom and tell the security guy you're there for me. I'll make sure he knows I'm expecting you."

His smoldering look told her precisely what he planned on doing to her when she got there.

She gulped. "Okay. I'll be there."

"Good." AJ dropped a quick kiss on her lips before heading for the door, but when he reached the threshold, he stopped and glanced over his shoulder. "And Brett?"

"Yeah?"

A darkly wicked note entered his voice. "Don't wear any panties."

Chapter Six

Thanks to AJ's parting words, Brett had a bitch of a time concentrating at work. Which probably wasn't something her clients would be thrilled to know, seeing as tattooing required patience and infinite concentration. One blunder could affect a person's entire life, whether it was a slip of the hand or one misspelled word. And sure, laser tattoo removal was commonplace nowadays, but Brett refused to put any of her clients through the process because of a careless mistake on her part.

So although her brain was in full-blown AJ mode, she'd forced herself to focus on making art and not think about how badly she wanted to have sex with him again.

By the time eight o'clock rolled around, the shop had emptied out, much to her delight. Once she'd finished touching up a back piece for her last client, she left her station and settled behind the front counter in the main room, doodling on a sketch pad as she waited for walk-ins. The monotonous buzzing behind the curtain of Rob's workspace served as a soundtrack for her sketching. She loved everything about working at the studio. The people, the smell of ink, the soothing sound of the tattoo gun.

But she'd love it even more if she were the one in charge, and not just another employee for her big brother to order around.

She lifted her head and glanced at the computer screensaver, which displayed a bright blue bubble flashing the current time. Eight ten. Argh. She couldn't take off until Rob gave her the okay, but she was dying to leap out of her chair and drive straight to Sin. She squirmed in her chair as she watched the minutes tick by, all the while keeping a constant vigil on the door and praying that nobody walked in demanding a last-minute consultation. The rule of thumb at Conlon Ink was to never turn a client away. Even if someone showed up five minutes to closing, Brett was expected to stay as late as necessary in order to tend to the customer.

Eight twelve. God, why was time dragging on so slowly? She was tempted to manually change the computer settings to nine o'clock and tell Rob her shift was over, but the new and improved Brett didn't pull stunts like that. Besides, Rob was too smart to buy such a dumb ploy.

Ding.

Brett smothered a groan when the bell over the door chimed loudly. She pasted on a smile, ready to greet the unwanted customer. When the door swung open, her unhappiness dissolved into relief.

"Hey, princess," her father said cheerfully. His heavy black boots thudded on the tiled floor as he strode to the counter. "C'mere and give your old man a hug."

Brett leaped out of the chair and walked into her dad's outstretched arms, returning the big hug he gave her. "Hey! What are you doing here?"

"Just came by to see my favorite daughter."

She rolled her eyes. "I'm your only daughter."

"Says who?" Jimmy Conlon flashed a sly smile. "Maybe I have a secret attic family I never told you about."

"Ha. Mom would've ripped your throat out with her bare hands if you pulled that crap on her."

"Never," he declared. "Your mother was a pacifist."

Hardly. Brett didn't have as many memories of her mom as she liked, but from what she did remember, Norah Conlon had been a total spitfire. Headstrong and outspoken, Brett's mom hadn't taken crap from anyone, and Brett knew she'd inherited her temper from her spirited mother.

As for her father, she might not have inherited his huge frame or tangle of red hair, but she'd definitely gotten her wild streak from him. She'd heard countless stories over the years about all the trouble he'd caused in the neighborhood growing up, thanks to his act-first-and-think-later nature. Once he'd married and had kids, he'd stopped solving problems with his fists, but he could still drink any of his sons under the table, and his boisterous personality charmed every person who sat in his tattoo chair.

Brett adored her father, but he could be so damn obstinate sometimes. It was probably due to his Irish blood, but man, his stubbornness was infuriating. He still viewed her as his little "princess," acted like she couldn't even brush her own teeth without his help. Granted, her past behavior had contributed to his inability to see her as a grown-up, but she wished he could at least acknowledge she was *trying* to change.

"Anyway, Rob told me you have a new boyfriend."

Brett's head swiveled in the direction of Rob's curtained-off station. Seriously? Already? She'd been working with her brother all day, and she certainly hadn't seen or heard him talking to their dad. Clearly he'd found a way to sneak in a phone call without her knowledge.

And people accused *women* of being gossips.

"Yeah, kind of," Brett answered, keeping her tone vague.

"It's still very new."

"Well, I don't need to meet the guy to know I approve." Her father looked beyond thrilled. "The Ten Grand Touchdown! Fuckin'-A! I can't believe he's coming to the house tomorrow. I'm making steak and garlic shrimp in his honor."

His enthusiasm would have made her laugh if she didn't feel so damn guilty. She hated deceiving her father, even more than she hated disappointing him.

She'd always been nothing but honest with her family, though her open-book mentality was probably one of the reasons she was forever on their shit lists. If she'd been a better—or more willing—liar, she wouldn't be in the boat she was currently in. Her family would be blissfully ignorant to all the immature things she'd done in the past. Her brothers wouldn't be on her case all the time.

Her father wouldn't have had to bail her out of jail last year…

The incident brought a clench of shame, along with a rush of anger, because she truly hadn't done anything wrong that night. Troy was the one who'd gotten plastered and picked a fight at the bar. Brett hadn't consumed a drop of alcohol, but when the brawl had escalated, the cops had carted her off with Troy and tossed her in the drunk tank right along with him.

God, the disapproving stare she'd received from her dad when he'd picked her up that night was still burned in her brain like a cattle brand. And she still remembered the sting of tears when he'd proceeded to blame *himself* for not "raising her right."

But he was so fucking wrong. After Brett's mother had died of cancer when Brett was seven, Jimmy Conlon had stepped up to the plate to raise their children. Dealing with the boys had been easy, but Brett knew he'd had a tough time relating to his only daughter. Her father was a man's man to the core, yet he'd done everything in his power to shower

Brett with the love and attention she'd craved. And all those girlie-girl activities she'd demanded they do together? God. He'd indulged her every whim, just so she wouldn't miss out on what the other girls her age were doing.

"Aw, what's this about?"

She jerked when she felt her dad's finger on her face. He gently brushed away the sheen of tears she hadn't even realized were there.

"Why are you crying, princess?" His brown eyes narrowed. "Did your new man do something to hurt you? Because if he did, I will break every bone in his body and—"

"No, of course not," she assured him, swallowing the lump of emotion obstructing her windpipe. "I was just thinking about all that girly stuff you used to do with me when I was a kid. You know, the tea parties, and playing dress up, and…" Her throat closed up again.

"Don't forget the Barbies," he said gruffly. "I sure haven't."

"You were such a good dad." She blinked away her tears. "You still are, you know."

Embarrassment colored his cheeks. "Where's this coming from, princess?"

"I don't know. The memories just popped into my head." She wiped her cheeks with the sleeve of her shirt, then shot a discreet look at the computer screen. Eight twenty-five. Damn.

"Got somewhere else to be?" her dad teased.

She was the one blushing now. "Kinda. I'm meeting AJ soon. He owns a nightclub downtown and I promised I'd stop by to visit him."

"Wide receiver *and* business owner? Shi-it. I like him even more now."

"*Just* a business owner. His football days are behind him," she said, then peeked at the clock again.

Her father chuckled. "Oh, get out of here already. You've

got one foot out the door as it is."

Brett answered in her most professional voice. "We don't close until nine, Dad. The job is my first priority."

"We won't go bankrupt if you cut out twenty minutes early. Besides, you've already been here ten hours." He ruffled her hair. "Go. I'll close up with your brother."

"Are you sure?" She didn't want to give him another reason to find fault in her, but he didn't seem bothered in the slightest.

"I'm sure. Go have fun."

With a burst of excitement, Brett grabbed her purse from the counter and made a dash to the door. "Thanks, Dad. I'll see you tomorrow."

"Don't forget to bring your man!" he called after her.

She stopped to toss him a grin. "Jeez. I think you love him more than you love me, and you haven't even met him."

"Ten grand, princess. Ten grand."

Brett was laughing as she hurried out of the shop. For all the headaches they gave her, her family was one of a kind. She was lucky to have them, which only made her feel worse that she hadn't lived up to their expectations in the past.

But that would change. She'd already eradicated any and all bad influences from her life—first and foremost being Troy. Their relationship had made her lose focus of what mattered to her, and she still wanted to kick herself for letting him take over her life the way he had. The jerk had used her for free tattoos and a place to crash, blinding her with his gorgeous looks and winning smile.

She wouldn't get fooled again. Nope, her next relationship was going to be with a man she could trust. Someone she could talk to, count on. Someone with *substance*.

Until then, she had three more weeks with AJ to look forward to. Three whole weeks to explore the mind-blowing sexual connection she hadn't seen coming.

And God, she couldn't wait to start exploring.

...

The male voice crackled through AJ's earpiece as he slid two bottles of Heineken across the counter to a customer.

"You've got a visitor," Jerry, who manned the club's security booth, informed him. "I sent her up to your office."

The way AJ's libido roared to life, you'd think Brett was standing naked in front of him instead of tucked away in his upstairs office. Last night should have been enough to satisfy the dark, restless urges for a while, but nope, twenty-four hours of pure, carnal fucking had barely scratched the surface.

He needed more, damn it.

Ignoring the ache down below, AJ headed to the register to make change for the customer. Then he signaled to Henry that he was ducking out and took off for the narrow staircase leading upstairs.

A glance over the railing revealed that Sin was already packed—a very encouraging sight, especially considering the night was still young. In the three years Sin had been in business, the club's clientele had tripled. These days, people lined up around the block to gain admittance, while Sin's owners happily reaped the rewards.

AJ had brought up the club's success to his father during their phone call earlier, hoping it might sway his parents' less than positive opinion about his line of work, but he shouldn't have bothered. No amount of bragging would convince them he'd made the right choice by not going to work with his dad. His stake in Sin was simply another black mark against him.

He shoved aside the reminder, not in the mood to fall into the guilt pit tonight. God knew he'd lived there every frickin' day of his life. He worked way too hard to be the son they needed him to be, and the thought brought a twinge of irony as he realized Brett was doing the same thing. Trying to meet the high expectations set upon her, but like him, she didn't quite fit in that saintly mold, either.

She wouldn't be there tonight if she had.

He reached the top of the stairs, his cock throbbing in anticipation as he zeroed in on his closed door. Christ, he'd never wanted a woman so badly before. The second he walked into that office, he had a better shot of winning the lottery than of restraining himself.

But why? Why didn't he feel the need to rein in that part of himself when he was with Brett? He had no answer for that, but he knew it was part of the reason he hadn't run screaming in the other direction when she'd dropped the boyfriend bomb earlier.

Hell, he'd pretend to be her *husband* as long as he got her naked again.

AJ was halfway down the hall when a familiar strawberry-blond head popped out of the neighboring office.

"Hey!" Darcy Grant broke out in a huge smile at the sight of him, quickly running up to throw her arms around him in a warm hug.

AJ pasted on a pleasant smile as he hugged her back. Though he'd never admit it to her or Reed, being around Darcy still brought a twinge of discomfort. Sure, he'd remained friends with most of his ex-girlfriends, but it was different with Darcy. She was dating his best friend now, which meant she was part of his life whether he liked it or not. The fact that he didn't have a choice in the matter grated slightly.

"How's it going?" she asked. "I haven't seen you around lately."

"Yeah, I've been at my folks' place a lot."

Her blue eyes went serious. "How's your mom doing?"

"Better. She's been taking it easy ever since the heart attack. My dad is doing his damndest to make sure she doesn't experience a second of stress. He's taken over the cooking, cleaning, pretty much whatever he can to make life easier for her."

Darcy nodded. "That's good. I keep meaning to drop by and visit her, but..." There was an awkward note in her voice. "I'm still not sure if it's, I don't know, appropriate, I guess."

"Why? Because we broke up?" he said lightly. "That doesn't matter, Darce. Mom would love to see you."

"Do they know I'm living with Reed now?"

AJ shook his head. "I don't talk about Reed much when I'm there. You know how they are."

She smiled wryly. "I'm not sure I blame them for disapproving of him. From what I've been told, he was a total troublemaker back in the day." She gestured to Reed's office door. "I just brought him some dinner. There's plenty of Chinese food to go around if you're hungry."

"Naah, I already ate, but thanks." His gaze strayed to the end of the hall again, but he tried not to reveal his impatience to Darcy.

They might be friends, but he definitely didn't want his ex-girlfriend knowing what he was up to tonight.

Hey, Darce, there's a hot chick in my office waiting for me to screw her senseless!

Yeah, he wasn't going there. He could already picture the look of disapproval that would grace Darcy's face, though he wasn't sure why it even mattered to him. Darcy was with Reed now. She had no say in his life and absolutely no right to judge him.

Still, his reluctance to reveal the fling only illustrated how much had been missing from his relationship with Darcy. Darcy was sweet and funny and wonderful, yet he'd always kept a part of himself hidden from her.

"Anyway, I'm sorry I can't stay and chat, but I have an important phone call to make."

"Is everything okay?" she said with concern.

"Yup. Just need to call one of our liquor suppliers."

The wary flicker in her eyes told him she didn't believe him, but he didn't particularly care at the moment. He'd already kept Brett waiting long enough.

As his impatience spilled over, he planted a brief kiss on Darcy's forehead before calling out a hasty good-bye on his way down the hall. He registered her bewildered response, but didn't turn around. A moment later, he was inside his office and locking the door behind him.

"Hi."

Brett instantly shot up from the visitor's chair and smoothed out her hair with one hand. She'd left it down tonight, and the silky black strands lingered right above her shoulders, providing him with a tantalizing view of her modest cleavage. She was wearing a silky black dress that stopped midthigh and the leather boots she'd had on yesterday, and with her tattooed arms exposed, she gave off a bad-girl vibe that he was totally digging.

And she hadn't been off base earlier—she *wasn't* his usual type. Normally he gravitated toward women like Darcy, girls with fresh-faced good looks, casual clothes, and down-to-earth personalities. Pixie bad-asses with ink hadn't played much of a role in his love life before now.

"Hi." He approached her slowly, stopping when they were two feet apart.

"So…" Brett cleared her throat. "Not to state the obvious or anything, but…I'm here."

"Did you do what I asked?"

"What you—oh." A crimson blush stained her cheeks. "Yes."

His cock twitched. "Show me."

Despite her beat of hesitation, there was no mistaking the flare of lust in her eyes.

Without breaking eye contact, she grasped the bottom of her dress and teasingly drew it up her thighs.

AJ's mouth went bone-dry as he watched the fabric slide higher and higher, revealing tantalizing glimpses of her smooth, fair skin. When the koi fish on her thigh became visible, he was hit with the memory of dragging his tongue over the tattoo while his fingers pumped inside her.

A groan slipped out as he focused on her bare sex. "Good girl," he rasped. "That's just what I wanted." She was about to let the dress drop when his hand flew up to stop her. "No, keep holding it up."

Her breasts rose as she sucked in a breath, but the material stayed bunched between her fingers.

"Spread your legs more," he ordered.

She widened her stance, exposing herself fully to his hungry gaze. His cock had turned into a slab of marble, pressing painfully into his zipper, but he didn't make a move to release it yet.

He'd never fucked a woman in his office before. He knew Gage and Reed got it on with Skyler and Darcy in their workspaces all the time, but AJ had always tried to act professional at work. Taking a woman on his desk would've felt like breaking the rules.

He was sick to death of rules.

"Walk over to the door," he said softly. "Brace your hands on it and bend over. Make sure your dress stays up."

Her breath caught. "What if I don't want to?"

"Then you don't get my cock." Slanting his head in challenge, he slid his hand down his abdomen and cupped himself over his pants.

Brett's eyes widened, lips parting seductively. Waves of arousal rolled off her slender body, and his own body responded in fervor, his erection thickening beneath his palm.

It occurred to him that they'd gone from *hi* to *spread*

your legs in five seconds flat, but that only made the whole encounter even hotter. She wasn't there so they could talk about their days.

She was there so they could make each other come.

Her breathing grew labored as she watched him rub the bulge in his pants. Then, without a single word, she walked to the door and did precisely what he'd commanded.

AJ chuckled. "That's what I thought."

He took a moment to admire the sexy-as-fuck picture she posed. Dark hair cascading down her back, high-heeled boots firmly planted on the ground, tight buttocks jutting out toward him.

Licking his lips, he came up behind her and cupped her bottom. Her flesh quivered beneath his palms, and when he squeezed, her entire body jerked. Chuckling again, he kept one hand on her ass and moved the other up to her breasts. He dipped his fingers beneath the neckline of her bodice and hissed through his teeth when he made contact with one naked breast. Christ, she hadn't been kidding about not wearing bras. His head spun like a carousel at the realization that she'd been buck naked underneath her dress.

AJ leaned in and brushed his lips over her ear. "Did you think about me when you were at work today?"

"Yes." Her voice was soft, shaky.

"Did you think about me touching you?"

"Yes."

He caressed her ass cheeks, then moved one finger between the crease and glided it lower, until the pad of it toyed with her opening. Moisture surrounded him. Holy hell. He couldn't wait to sink his cock into that hot, wet paradise.

"Did you think about *me*?" She twisted her head, bold curiosity gleaming in those amazing brown-black eyes.

A thrill shot up his spine. Each time this woman looked at him, he got the feeling she was actually *seeing* him. *Him*, and not the man he tried to be half the time. There was something seriously exciting about that. Something dark and erotic and unbelievably freeing.

"Well, did you?" she demanded when he didn't respond.

"Every fucking second."

He slipped the tip of his finger into her core and enjoyed the way she whimpered.

"I thought about doing this," he rasped.

He pushed his finger deeper inside her.

"And *this*."

He fingered her slowly.

"And *this*."

He increased the tempo, pumping hard enough to make her cry out.

"I've been walking around with a hard-on all day, thinking about all the things I want to do to this sweet pussy."

To prove it, he pressed his groin against her ass and rotated his hips, letting her feel every hard inch of him.

She moaned. "You're such a tease."

"Am I?" he said mockingly. "Hmmm. Does that mean you want me to stop?"

Brett cursed as he abruptly withdrew his finger. She spun around, a mixture of passion and agony flashing in her eyes. "I want you inside me."

Despite the incessant throbbing of his cock, AJ managed a reckless grin. "Good. Because that's exactly where I want to be."

He nudged her back into position, idly toying with her clit as he reached into his pocket for the condom he'd stashed there. He didn't take off his pants, just shoved them low enough to free his cock and then eased the blunt head into her opening. No foreplay needed—she was wetter than ever, so visibly aroused AJ knew she was more than ready for him.

He gripped her hips with both hands and plunged inside,

filling her to the hilt. Pleasure crashed into him, the sensation so intense he swayed on his feet and had to take a second to blink through the black dots swimming in his vision.

Holy hell. He'd never felt anything like this before. Fierce need, acute pleasure. And, oddly enough, a sense of peace. He didn't have to wear the good-guy mask with Brett. He could take her right here against this door, and to hell with anyone on the other side of it.

He shuddered when she wiggled her ass in an attempt to thrust backward against him. "Fuck me," she pleaded hoarsely. "Please."

His pulse sped up. So did his tempo. With every thrust and retreat of his hips, he drove deeper and harder inside her, giving in to the primal urge to claim her. Their heavy breathing and the sound of flesh slapping flesh echoed in the air, a wicked soundtrack to their wicked joining.

AJ dug his fingers into her hips and sealed their bodies tighter together. "*Fuck*. Feels so damn good," he choked out, his head falling in the crook of her neck.

He kissed her, tasted her, inhaled her. The scent of roses and lavender filled his nostrils, a fragrance that seemed almost too sweet for a woman wearing leather fuck-me boots and covered in tattoos.

His mouth traveled up the graceful column of her throat toward her ear. As he sucked gently on her earlobe, he slowed down, enjoying the spectacular sensation of sliding in and out of her tight sheath.

"No," she blurted out. "Faster. Harder, damn it."

"No." He teased her earlobe with his tongue. One hand left her waist to circle her body, lazily seeking out her clit. The second he made contact, she bucked like a wild horse and let out a tormented moan.

"I like you like this." His mouth abandoned her ear to whisper into the nape of her neck, the baby-fine hairs there tickling his lips. "Pinned against the wall, letting me take you from behind. I can't see your eyes, but I can picture the look on your face. Hazy, desperate… Are you desperate, angel?"

"No, I'm *angry*." She gave another backward thrust, her inner muscles bearing down on his cock as if to trap him inside her. "You're talking too much when you should be *making me come*."

AJ laughed at her impatience. He threaded his fingers through her hair, then tugged hard to twist her head toward him. The sight of her nearly did him in. Cheeks flushed and eyes glazed with desperation, just as he'd predicted.

A sense of power washed over him, a jolt of adrenaline he'd only ever experienced in an MMA cage. He'd been with lots of women. Women who wanted him, women who loved every damn thing he did to them, but it had never been like this. Brett's face conveyed naked passion that made his heart race. She didn't hide a thing from him. She was raw and uninhibited and had no problem telling him—no, *showing* him—exactly what she wanted.

Except…he suddenly wanted something else tonight.

The relentless need to come had been replaced by a stronger one—the urge to control. To push their boundaries.

Releasing a slow, unsteady breath, he slid out of her body and removed the condom.

"What are you doing?" She was practically wailing, shock and disbelief etched into her pretty features. "Why are you stopping?"

"I'm trying something out." He tossed the condom in the wastebasket near the door and tucked his monster erection back into his pants. "I want you to go home."

Brett stayed rooted in place, her dress still bunched around her waist, her jaw wide open. "Are you kidding me? You want me to go *home*? *Now*? Are you *insane*?"

The fire in her eyes brought a rueful grin to his lips.

"Probably," he admitted.

Probably? Nuh-uh. Try *absolutely*. His cock was as angry with him as Brett was, poking so hard into his zipper that he wouldn't be surprised if it bore the impression of tiny metal teeth marks.

"But I'm interested in conducting an experiment," he finished. "Call it an exercise in anticipation if you want."

"Yeah? Well, you can take your exercise and shove it up your butt!"

He ignored her enraged shout and took another step back. "One more thing," he added.

"You can take your 'one more thing' and *shove it up your butt*!"

A laugh popped out. "Stop threatening to put things in my ass and listen." He folded his arms over his chest. "When you get home tonight, you're not allowed to touch yourself."

"*Excuse me*?" She glared daggers at him.

"I mean it," he said sternly. "If you come, I'll know."

Her mouth closed. Then opened again. Then closed. "Oh my God. I'm *this close* to punching you in the face right now, you know that? *You* invited *me* here tonight, *you're* throwing *me* out, and now you're telling me what I can or can't do when I get home?"

"Yup."

"You are unbelievable." She charged forward, her dress fluttering over her thighs, effectively covering her from view. "This isn't cool," she snapped, her cheeks redder than a fire engine. "I'm dying here. I *want* this."

"And you'll get it." He smirked. "Tomorrow."

"No way. We either finish this now, or we don't finish it at all."

"We'll finish it." He offered a careless shrug. "Tomorrow."

Brett gaped at him. He'd never seen a woman look more livid, and maybe it made him a total jackass, but he was kind of digging the whole I'm-going-to-murder-you vibes she was throwing off.

Just meant it would be all the more explosive when he finally gave them what they both craved.

"Oh, what time should we go to your dad's house tomorrow?"

She stared at him as if he'd just confessed to strangling her cat. "We? *We*? You're living in a dream world if you think that's ever—" She stopped abruptly, every breath coming out as a harsh pant. "Listen up, AJ—what the hell does AJ stand for, anyway?"

"Adam James," he said helpfully.

She marched up and jabbed him right between the pecs with her index finger. "Listen up, *Adam James*, you can't just…just…*blueball* me—"

He choked down a laugh.

"—and then expect me to be all sunshine and rainbows and sparkly silver unicorns! And you know what? I don't need you to be my boyfriend anymore. I'll just tell my family that you ended up being a total jerk—and guess what, dude, it won't even be a lie!"

She stomped to the desk to grab her purse, shoved the strap over her shoulder, and stomped back to the door.

"I am so frickin' pissed right now," she announced. "And FYI? After I get home and finish constructing a voodoo doll of you? I'm going to make myself come a million times. No, a *gazillion* times."

He arched one brow. "No, you won't."

"Don't you dare give me that smug, self-righteous look. I'm not playing your little mind games, okay?" She flung open the door. "Have yourself a good night, AJ."

"I'll see you tomorrow," he called after her.

"No, you won't," she said without turning around.

He was still smiling as she flew out the door.

Chapter Seven

"Hey, you made it!" Rob said happily, his dark eyes focused on the man who'd just strolled through the back gate like he owned the place.

Oh no he di-int.

Brett's jaw hit the freshly mowed lawn of her father's backyard as her gaze collided with AJ.

AJ.

Frickin' *AJ*.

Disbelief, anger, and an infuriating burst of joy erupted inside her as the man who'd tormented her yesterday approached the patio table where she sat with her dad and brothers. What the hell was he *doing* here? She'd made herself clear last night. So clear she might as well have hired a plane to write the words in the sky—their arrangement was over. Kaput. Dunzo. After the stunt he'd pulled, she wanted nothing more to do with the jerk.

Liar. Of course you do.

Brett silenced the internal voice, choosing instead to shoot her deepest, meanest scowl in AJ's direction. When she noticed how good he looked, her irritation only doubled. The guy was wearing *khakis*, for Pete's sake, all preppy-like with his white T-shirt and flawless blond hair and clean-shaven jaw. She wasn't supposed to find him appealing, damn it. The boy-next-door type had never done it for her in the past.

Boy next door. The description lingered in her head, triggering the urge to snort aloud. Ha. Boy next door, her ass. AJ Walsh was the *devil*.

She still couldn't believe he'd lured her to the club last night, brought her to the orgasmic edge, and then asked her to *leave*. All so he could indulge in his little—what had he called it? Right. An exercise in anticipation.

Well, double ha. He'd been on a power trip, plain and simple. He'd wanted to see how far and how hard he could push her, and if there was one thing Brett Conlon didn't appreciate, it was being pushed around.

"Sorry, I'm late," AJ told the group. "My GPS took me on a crazy route. It doesn't seem to understand what *one-way street* means."

"Well, I'm glad you found the place all right," Rob said, sticking out his arm so the two men could exchange a fist bump.

"I thought you had to work," Brett spoke up tightly, her cloudy expression leaving no doubt as to how she felt about this unwanted intrusion.

"Nope, turns out Reed and Gage can handle the inventory on their own," he answered, his lie coming out as effortlessly as hers. "I tried to call you for directions, but I think your phone's dead. So I grabbed Rob's cell number off the Conlon Ink website, and luckily he got back to me quick-fast."

"Yes, how lucky," she muttered.

Brett set down the burger she'd been holding. Her appetite had vanished. She felt like diving out of her chair and kicking AJ in the shin, but the new Brett wasn't allowed to lose her temper. Especially when her father was gazing at AJ with blatant approval.

Her dad raised his massive body out of his chair and extended a hand. "Jimmy Conlon. And you must be the man who's dating my daughter."

"Yes, sir. I'm AJ."

"Can it with this *sir* business. Call me Jimmy."

The two men exchanged a hearty handshake, and unlike Brett's previous boyfriends, AJ didn't seem the least bit intimidated by her father's size.

At six four, with his bushy red beard, muscular chest, and multitude of tattoos, her dad painted an imposing picture. God knew Troy had been scared shitless the first time he'd seen him.

"Nice to meet you, Jimmy," AJ said easily. "I hear I made you some money back in the day."

Jimmy's mouth stretched in a wide grin. "Ten grand, son. You helped pay off the mortgage."

AJ grinned back. "Glad I could be of assistance." He turned to the other two men at the large, round table. "Jordan, right?" he said to the younger one. "I remember you from high school."

Jordan didn't get up, but leaned forward to shake AJ's hand. "I remember you too. You were lightning fast on that football field."

Brett's oldest brother, Mike, rounded out the introductions, and Brett couldn't help but marvel at the sight of AJ surrounded by the men in her family. Every Conlon male was inked up, had facial hair, and stood well over six feet tall. AJ was around Jordan's size at six one, but next to her dad and brothers, he looked like a rich pretty boy who'd gotten lost on his way to the country club and accidentally wandered into their backyard.

Come to think of it, he probably *was* rich. Brett had no

idea where he'd grown up, but he didn't look like someone who hailed from Southie.

Yet strangely enough, he seemed to fit right in. Brett had to swallow her amazement as AJ chatted with her dad and brothers as if he'd known them for years. He readily accepted a bottle of Bud Light from Rob, along with the burger and shrimp plate her dad handed him.

Brett let the casual interaction go on for several minutes before she'd had enough. She hadn't invited him, damn it!

Okay, well, technically she had, but then she'd *uninvited* him. The guy had a lot of nerve showing up after he'd left her high and dry last night.

Or maybe high and *wet* was the more apt description.

"I want to give AJ a tour of the house," she announced.

The men stopped talking. Her dad shot her a quizzical look before speaking in a wry voice. "The man's just sitting down to eat, princess. He can take the tour later."

"No, it's okay," AJ intervened, setting his plate on the table. "I wouldn't mind seeing the house my angel grew up in."

His angel?

Oh, hell no.

Brett grabbed AJ's hand and dragged him to the sliding door that led into the kitchen. "I can't wait for you to see it," she said through clenched teeth.

After she'd closed the door behind them, she bulldozed past the kitchen and marched toward the hall, not bothering to see if he was following.

He was. But he had the good sense to keep three feet of distance between them as they squared off in the hall.

"What the hell!" Brett blurted out. "I told you the arrangement was off."

His lips twitched. "I decided to call your bluff."

"It wasn't a bluff. I meant every frickin' word."

"I know I left you hurting, but if it helps, I was hurting just as bad." He ruefully glanced at his crotch.

Brett's traitorous eyes lowered, and her breath hitched when she noticed his unmistakable hard-on.

"Good. You deserve to hurt." Irritation bubbled inside her, along with indignation over what he'd done last night. Depriving her of an orgasm like that. Asshole. "I can't believe you just stopped," she muttered.

"I told you why I did."

"Mmm-hmmm. Your bullshit anticipation excuse."

"It wasn't an excuse." He took a step toward her. "The anticipation is half the fun, baby. The hunger…that burning ache of wanting something so badly but not being able to take it…"

The air in the hallway got hotter. Thickened with awareness.

AJ inched closer, slow and purposeful, effectively backing her into the wall. Her butt bumped into solid drywall. She had nowhere to go.

She found herself staring at his mouth. The sensual curve of it, the surprisingly full bottom lip. She had to bite the inside of her cheek to stop from acting on the impulse to kiss him.

"Did you make yourself come last night?" he murmured.

"Yes." She shot him a haughty look. "Many times."

"Liar." He lifted his finger to her face and traced the seam of her lips. "You wouldn't be this tense if you had."

Brett gritted her teeth. "I'm tense because you crashed our barbecue. I told you I didn't want you to come."

"Bullshit. You do want me to come." The silky note in his voice told her he wasn't talking about the barbecue. "I want you to come, too." His eyes grew heavy-lidded. "I wanted to feel your orgasm squeezing my cock last night."

"But you stopped," she reminded him in accusation.

"I stopped," he agreed.

His hand drifted down to the waistband of her jeans.

Brett's heart skipped a beat. "What are you doing?" she squeaked.

AJ didn't answer. He popped open the button and pulled the zipper down, then slipped his hand inside. Her sex instantly clenched beneath his warm palm. She involuntarily rubbed against it, and God, it felt so good she almost keeled over.

Her body was hypersensitive from the lack of relief she'd given it yesterday, her clit swollen to the point of pain. She knew AJ could feel how damp her panties were, but she was too turned on to care.

He stroked her gently, the heel of his hand teasing her clit and unleashing a flurry of shivers. Her eyelids fluttered closed as she melted into his skillful touch.

"And I'm going to stop now, too."

Brett's eyes flew open. "What?"

"I'm going to take you to the edge again. And then yank you right back."

God, she was already close. Just a tiny bit more pressure and she'd come apart, so hard she'd probably see stars.

But the pressure didn't come. AJ withheld it from her, continuing to brush her clit with featherlight caresses.

"And after lunch?" he went on. "I'll find another reason to get you alone, and I'll do it again." He drew a teasing circle around her clit. "By the time this day is over, you're going to want me so bad you won't be able to breathe. You won't be able to walk without feeling that burn between your legs."

"Neither will you." Smirking, she cupped his impressive package over his jeans and squeezed hard.

A tormented sound escaped his lips. "Oh, I'll be feeling the same burn, baby. I'm going to be aching for you."

"Then why?" she demanded in frustration. "Why are you torturing us?"

"Anticipation," he said again. "Think about how good it will be when we finally let go. Like a slow burning fuse, getting hotter and hotter...and then"—he brought his mouth to her neck and nipped at her feverish flesh— "when it explodes..."

"Bang," she whispered.

"Oh yeah. Bang," he echoed, low and seductive. "You're gonna come so hard tonight, Brett. So hard you'll scream."

He lightly pinched her clit, and her entire body jerked.

In the blink of an eye, his hand disappeared.

"Now let's go back outside." He smiled. "My food is getting cold."

• • •

Torture.

That was the only word to describe what he was putting his body through. The cuts and bruises and bloody noses he'd endured during his fighting days were nothing compared to the pain AJ was feeling right now. Every muscle was strung tight, every drop of blood pulsing in his groin so that he not only felt horny, but light-headed.

Delaying climax had seemed like a good idea last night. Today, AJ just wanted to punch his own jaw for coming up with such an excruciating plan.

Fortunately, Brett's family proved to be a good distraction from the dull ache. Her brothers were a laugh riot, regaling him with stories about their lives and their work at the family tattoo parlors, while her father barraged him with questions about his own life. He felt like he was on the witness stand at times, but Jimmy Conlon's laid-back attitude and contagious sarcasm made the whole interrogation process surprisingly fun.

Eventually, the conversation shifted to sports, which didn't surprise him, seeing as there was a Patriots banner hanging over the sliding door. The Conlon men were football nuts, and soon they were throwing out statistics and making predictions for the upcoming season like they were ESPN correspondents.

As the sports talk dragged on, AJ noticed that Brett's expression had completely glazed over. She'd found a pen and sketchpad somewhere, and was in the process of doodling what looked like an elephant wearing ice skates and a teeny crown.

AJ had to chuckle as he glanced over her shoulder at her handiwork. "I think we're boring Brett," he announced to the guys.

Rob gave a careless shrug. "Ah, she's used to it."

"Doesn't make it *right*," Brett muttered under her breath.

AJ experienced a pang of sympathy as Jimmy and his boys went back to chatting without a single look at Brett. Obviously it was a common occurrence for her, but he still felt bad watching her sit on the sidelines while her family ignored her.

Though it made sense now, her single-minded determination to show her family she'd changed. But he also wondered if her attempts at pleasing them had less to do with the tattoo parlor she wanted to run, and more about wanting her family to pay attention to her. To *notice* her.

He, on the other hand, found it impossible *not* to notice her. His gaze tracked her like a missile as she went to the cooler to grab a beer. Dark blue jeans hugged her ass and a loose cardigan covered her arms, which was a damn shame. Her tattoos were too spectacular to hide.

They'd slept together less than forty-eight hours ago, yet it suddenly felt like an eternity since he'd last seen her naked. His cock went semi hard as he imagined stripping her clothes off and licking every inch of her body again.

He gave his growing erection a silent reprimand, then walked over to Brett and rested his hand on the small of her back. "I like your family," he confessed. "They're a lot of fun."

Brett's gaze shifted across the yard to where Rob and Mike were engaged in a loud argument about the benefits of a nickel defense.

"They're okay, I guess," she said grudgingly. Then she smiled. "My brothers can be a pain in the ass, but at least they've always got my back. Do you have any siblings?"

His shoulders tensed. "No."

The second the word left his mouth, guilt exploded in his gut. Fuck. It felt like a betrayal to Joey's memory to deny his existence.

"When I was growing up I used to wish I was an only child," Brett said, oblivious to his current state of turmoil. "I felt like my dad gave so much attention to my brothers, and not enough for me. I wanted him all to myse—"

"I had a brother," he blurted out.

She froze. "What? But you just said—"

"He died," AJ admitted, swallowing a lump of pain. "So technically, I *don't* have any siblings. But I used to."

Her voice softened. "I'm sorry. How did he die?"

It was difficult to answer when his throat had closed up to the point of suffocation. "Accident," he mumbled. "And not something I want to get into right now."

To his relief, Brett rerouted her line of questioning. "What was he like?"

Bitterness promptly joined the eddy of emotions in his stomach. "He was perfect."

She offered a wry look. "Nobody's perfect."

"Trust me, Joey was. Football star, straight-A student, perfect manners, hero complex. He followed the rules, didn't get into trouble, charmed everyone he met. My parents worshipped the ground he walked on."

"How old were you when he died?"

"Eight. He was sixteen."

"That's a pretty big age difference." She paused. "It makes sense that you think he was perfect. Little kids always put their older siblings on a pedestal. But your parents must be really proud of you, too. You own a successful club, you fought professionally, and probably made tons of money…"

His chest had gone so stiff he was surprised his ribs didn't crack when he drew a breath. "They're not too thrilled about Sin, and they were even less thrilled about the fighting." Before she could respond, he rapidly changed the subject. "Why isn't your mom around, if you don't mind me asking?"

Brett's expression went sad. "She died of breast cancer when I was seven."

"Ah, shit. I'm sorry to hear that. Were you two close?"

"Yeah. I was her little girl and she spoiled me rotten. Said I deserved it since I had to grow up surrounded by those three idiots." Brett raised her voice as she gestured to her brothers.

"I heard that," Jordan shouted.

"You were supposed to," Brett shouted back. Grinning, she reached for AJ's hand and gave it a little tug. "Come on, let's go see what these boneheads are arguing about."

The second their skin made contact, heat spread through his body in long, pulsing waves. "Actually, I think I'd like another tour," he drawled. "You didn't show me the upstairs last time."

Her breath caught when he rubbed his thumb over the center of her palm. "You wouldn't," she said, her voice barely above a whisper.

"Wouldn't what? Keep tormenting you?" He chuckled softly. "But I promised you I would—and I always keep my promises. I'm going to tease you all day, angel. All. Fucking. Day."

She visibly swallowed. "You're evil."

"Damn straight." He stroked her wrist, then laced their fingers together and turned to address the Conlons. "Excuse us for a second. Brett wants to show me some of her old drawings…"

AJ stayed true to his word. For the next two hours, he found three more excuses to get Brett alone. Three more opportunities to coax her to the edge of orgasm before cruelly wrenching her back. By the time they were preparing to leave, she looked ready to explode, which would have been funny if he weren't hovering over the same lust-filled powder keg. He just hoped her family hadn't noticed how many times he'd had to rearrange the front of his pants. He doubted it, seeing as they'd been bickering about sports, cars, and tattoos the whole time.

Despite their three-track minds, though, he'd genuinely enjoyed hanging out with the Conlons. They were entertaining, interesting, and incredibly easy to talk to.

But AJ was tired of talking. It was time to put him and Brett out of their misery before they both went up in flames.

Since Brett had arrived in her own car, they drove to her apartment separately, and even the act of pressing his foot on the gas pedal made his cock ache. Miraculously, he managed to make it to Brett's place without coming in his pants.

As he hopped out of the Jeep, he was greeted by the scent of garlic and ginger wafting from the Korean general store. The door had been propped open by a milk crate to let the fresh spring air in, the same warm breeze that brushed AJ's bare arms like a teasing caress.

When Brett's car pulled up behind his, his pulse took off in a gallop. Christ, he wasn't leaving her side until both of them were sated and sweaty and limp from pleasure. The club didn't open until seven and he'd already told his bartenders he might show up late, so he had nothing but time on his hands.

He planned on taking advantage of every damn second.

"Upstairs. Now," he commanded when Brett met him at the curb.

"Yes, sir," she said with a mock salute, but he didn't miss the impatience in her gait as they climbed the stairs to her apartment.

This was his second visit to Brett's domain, and he found it as soothing as the first. With its funky mismatched furniture and dozens of colorful paintings on the walls, her place was so much more welcoming than his. Her style was an odd mix of modern and antique, and so frickin' cozy it brought a pang of longing to his gut.

His own apartment was neat, sterile, and bland. He hadn't had the heart to say no to his mother when she'd insisted on decorating it, but he couldn't deny that her efforts had succeeded in making him feel like an intruder in his own home.

"Bedroom." Brett's voice sliced through his thoughts.

He narrowed his eyes when he noticed the look on her face. Stern and steely, a sure sign that she was up to something.

Deciding to humor her, he headed down the hall, and when they entered her bedroom, she pointed to the bed. "Lie down."

AJ raised one eyebrow. "You're bossing me around now?"

"Damn straight." She lifted an eyebrow in return. "Did you think I was going to let you get away with what you did last night? And what you did today? You really don't know me at all, *Adam James*."

No, he really didn't, but he sure as hell was enjoying getting to know her. He loved the fire simmering beneath her surface, the way she wasn't afraid to speak her mind. He'd already caught several glimpses of her temper, already learned firsthand that it didn't take much for it to spill over, but he liked that about her. Brett Conlon was full of *life*, and damned if he didn't admire that.

It was almost a shame she'd decided to rein in that fire in order to please her family. AJ much preferred this scorching, passionate side of her.

She fluttered a hand at the mattress again. "Lie. Down."

He sauntered over to the bed and stretched out on top of the quilted bedspread, propping his hands behind his head as he watched Brett march toward the closet. She leaned inside and disappeared in the row of hanging clothes, making mysterious rustling sounds as she rummaged around.

When she turned to face him, she held a silk necktie in each hand.

"Are we playing dress up?" AJ said casually.

"Nope." Her expression turned downright wicked as she approached the foot of the bed. "Take off your shirt."

He sat up and yanked on the collar of his T-shirt, peeling the material over his head. Brett's eyes darkened with approval when his bare chest was exposed, and man, knowing his body turned her on was a goddamn ego boost.

Her hips swayed seductively as she joined him on the bed. She gave him a forceful shove so he was on his back again, then climbed on top of him and straddled his crotch.

Fuuuuck.

The intimate contact turned his dick to stone, and his hips involuntarily rose so he could rub up against her. The friction was so insanely mind-blowing he almost blacked out, but a sharp tug on his left wrist snapped him back to reality.

He eyed her warily. "What are you doing?"

Rather than answer, she looped one tie around his wrist, then wrenched his arm up and aligned his hand with one of the bedposts. He didn't protest as she secured his wrist to the post. He was far too fascinated.

"This"—she fashioned an impressive-looking knot and pulled hard—"is what I like to call payback."

A second later, he was tied to her bed.

Chapter Eight

Brett was proud of her handiwork as she tested AJ's bindings—and slightly surprised that he'd allowed her to do it without a single objection.

"Payback, huh?" he echoed. "Whatcha gonna do, Brett? Spank me? 'Cause I'd have to roll over for that, and I'm afraid I'm a bit tied up at the moment."

She snorted. "Ha-ha, hilarious. And please, don't tempt me—you totally deserve a spanking for the way you tormented me."

Her hand lowered to his waist to toy with the button of his khakis. She deliberately grazed her knuckles over the ridge of his very obvious erection, enjoying the way his abdomen tightened as he sucked in a breath. His chest was truly wonderful. An endless expanse of smooth golden skin, lightly dusted with dark blond hair and rippling with power.

"You should get some ink," she mused, skimming her fingers over his defined pectoral muscles.

His hot male flesh quivered beneath her touch. "Yeah?"

"Oh yeah." She traced one flat nipple, then bent forward

to flick her tongue against it.

AJ groaned.

"Most MMA fighters I've seen on TV have tats," she remarked. "How come you never got any?"

His features had grown taut, a sheen of moisture appearing on his forehead as she teased both his nipples with her fingers. When he spoke, his voice came out strained, distracted. "There was never anything I considered important enough to permanently put on my body."

"Pity." She kissed the patch of hair between his pecs, then followed the wispy line down to his groin.

"Jesus," he mumbled. "I'm totally digging this payback, baby."

"You won't for much longer. I haven't even gotten started yet." She smiled sweetly. "I'm going to torture you, *baby*."

"Yeah?" He didn't seem too concerned by the threat.

"Oh yeah. Like I said, I don't like being dicked around."

He blinked innocently. "Really? I happen to enjoy it." His lower body rose off the mattress, his thick erection bumping her hand. "Dick me around, Brett. Please."

She swallowed a laugh. God, this man never failed to surprise her. All the memories she had of him from high school, all the assumptions…flawed, each and every one of them.

The AJ Walsh she'd admired walking the halls of Hawthorne High had been a fantasy. The man she'd spent the weekend with? He was *real*. He was playful and sexy and far more dominant than she'd ever expected. In fact, if Troy or any of her former boyfriends had bossed her around the way AJ did, she probably would've slapped them upside the head. But for some reason, she totally got off on AJ's bossiness.

Of course, being the one in charge also had its benefits.

As she undid his pants and freed his erection, a sense of power she'd never experienced surged through her veins.

With his hands secured to the bedposts, he was completely at her mercy. She could do whatever she wanted to him, and he was helpless to stop her.

She stroked his shaft, enjoying the weight of him, the smooth, hot flesh beneath her fingers. He was long and thick, hard as a rock, and soft as velvet. She could see his pulse throbbing in his cock as she moved her fist in long, leisurely strokes.

"Best payback ever." AJ moaned as he thrust into her hand.

"You still think so, huh? Then I guess you've forgotten about all those times you got me close today and then took your hand away." She flashed a devious look. "But I sure haven't. PS—I'm going to do the same thing to you now." She nodded at his immobile hands. "And there's not a damn thing you can do about it."

Smirking, Brett leaned over and swiped her tongue along the tiny slit on his engorged head, licking the drop of salty moisture pooled there.

He jerked on the bed, wrists smacking the posts as he tried to move his arms.

"Don't waste your time," she said helpfully. "Fun fact—my dad and brothers are avid fishermen. Every summer we take our boat out to the Finger Lakes for a two-week fishing trip. Which means I know my knots." She beamed at him. "I tie a mean bowline, if I do say so myself."

AJ made an unintelligible sound. His features contorted in agony when she gave his erection a teasing squeeze. Then she licked him again, a slow circle around the crown of his cock, and a strangled groan tore out of his throat. She peered up and encountered the sexiest sight on earth. AJ in full-blown arousal mode—lips parted, cheeks flushed, strong throat working as he swallowed repeatedly.

Her sexual tormenting continued in the form of

featherlight licks up and down his shaft, each delicate flick of the tongue summoning another anguished noise from him. When she decided to take pity on him by sucking on his tip, he shuddered as if she'd dumped a bucket of cold water over his head.

Brett lifted her head with a mocking chuckle. "You doing okay?"

"What do you think?" he croaked.

"I think I'm going to let you come." She firmly wrapped her hand and lips around him, pumping hard as she tightened the suction of her mouth.

Five strokes, six, seven…and just as she felt his body tense up, she released him with a *pop* and leaned back on her elbows.

"Actually, no," she said cheerfully. "I changed my mind."

The expletive he let out was so loud and tortured she choked on a giggle.

"Oh, I'm sorry, what was that?"

"I hate you," he mumbled.

"No, you don't." She cupped his sac and fondled it lightly. His cock had gone impossibly thicker, resting on his navel and pleading for attention.

Oh yeah. This was power, all right. She had AJ Walsh right where she wanted him, and he wouldn't get an ounce of relief until *she* decided to give it to him. How many orgasms had he deprived her of already? She quickly did the math—one last night, at least three today.

She had a lot of work to do.

For the next thirty minutes, she showed him exactly what she thought of his blasted anticipation. Her soft licks and teasing pumps, intermixed with greedy sucking and the hard squeezing of his balls, turned the man on her bed into a cursing, trembling mess of need. And all the while, Brett gauged his responses with delight, until she knew his body better than she knew her own.

When his six-pack tightened and his balls drew up, it meant he was close.

When he wheezed as if all the oxygen had drained from his lungs, it meant he needed more.

When his bound hands thrashed against the bedposts, it meant he was losing his frickin' mind.

The third time she took him to the brink, his release nearly breached the surface, and only the fast, sharp squeeze of her hand managed to ward it off.

AJ grunted, but there wasn't an ounce of pain in his eyes. Just smoky pleasure and unadulterated lust. He was no longer fighting the knots, either. He actually seemed to be enjoying the complete lack of control.

"You like this," she marveled when she saw his face.

"Fuck yeah," he growled.

Brett wondered if she would like it if their roles were reversed. If *she* was the one at AJ's mercy.

The answer was swift and unequivocal: God, yes. She'd love every dirty second of it.

Releasing him, she inhaled a wobbly breath and slid off the bed. She didn't say a word as she stripped off her clothes. Just kicked each garment away until she stood naked in front of him.

AJ's gaze smoldered as it roamed her body. "Payback's over?"

"Are you kidding me?" She stuck out her tongue. "It's time for round two."

If she managed to survive it.

Every muscle in her body was coiled tighter than a rattlesnake, every nerve ending crackling with sexual energy. She was wet and achy and *so* damn ready, but she'd set a course of action, and she intended to follow through on it.

Round two entailed the same level of teasing as Round

One, only this time she brought her own body into play. This time when she bent over, it was to rub her nipples over his cock—and this time, they were *both* groaning with abandon.

God. She was torturing herself now, and she wasn't sure she was capable of the same awe-inspiring patience AJ seemed to possess in spades.

She straddled him again, more for her sake than his, because the feel of his cock rubbing her aching clit was absolute heaven.

"Holy hell, that's hot." The intensity of his expression made her shiver. "Keep doing that."

She gripped his erection and rubbed the blunt head over her sensitive bud, until his shaft was slick from her juices and her clit was so swollen it hurt.

Struggling for breath, she eased backward. One hand stayed on his cock but went motionless, while the other traveled between her legs. Although AJ had a perfect view of what she was doing, she didn't feel vulnerable or exposed. If anything, the hungry gaze fixed on her core only fueled her arousal.

When she rubbed her clit with her index finger, he growled again. "Christ. That's it…touch yourself."

Her knees parted as she slipped one finger inside, and his eyes burned with lust.

"I bet you wish it was your finger inside me right now, don't you?" She grinned. "Do you want me to tell you how wet I am?"

"I can see how wet you are," he rumbled, tracking the movements of her hand. There was no mistaking the moisture shining on her finger.

Another surge of feminine power coursed through her. Whoa. He was looking at her like she was a treasure chest and he held the map to unlocking it. His erection pulsed and twitched against her hand, but rather than give it what it craved, she let go altogether.

With one finger lodged inside her, she used her other hand to tend to her clit.

Oh crap. She was getting close.

"Don't," he commanded when he noticed her trembling. "You're not allowed to come. Not until you're sitting on my dick."

"Wow. Still issuing orders even when you're tied up. You've got some balls."

He glanced at his crotch, smug and unashamed. "Yup. Big ones. How about you put your mouth on them again?"

Brett smothered a laugh. "Maybe later."

She eased the pressure of her fingers, lightly stroking herself. God, she wanted him inside her. It was all she'd been thinking about ever since he'd ordered her to leave last night.

When she was no longer convinced she could stop her impending orgasm, she withdrew her fingers and reached for him again. Her hand was slippery from her arousal, making it easy to glide her fist up and down his shaft.

AJ took one look at his glistening erection—and lost it.

"No more." The desperate words ripped out of his throat. "Get up here and ride me, or I'll break this goddamn bed to splinters trying to get loose."

It would have been fun to torment him a bit longer, but her patience had disappeared like a puff of smoke. Brett left the bed only to find a condom, then climbed back on his lap and hurriedly rolled the latex over his shaft.

Rather than guide him inside her, she leaned forward so one nipple brushed his lips. AJ sucked without hesitation, his eager tongue lashing the rigid bud as he drew it deep in his mouth. Lord, even tied up, the man was fully capable of setting her body on fire, and as a sizzle of electricity zinged from her nipple to her core, Brett had no illusions about who was in charge.

He might be on his back, but AJ Walsh was in complete

control. He had been from the start.

Her nipple was still in his mouth when she impaled herself on him, and the wild groan he let out vibrated in her breasts and sent shivers up her spine.

"Sweet Jesus, Brett. Fuck me. *Now*."

She couldn't have denied him even if she'd wanted to. Her body moved of its own volition, grinding against him in a frantic rhythm.

AJ lasted four strokes.

She lasted five.

The orgasm was unlike any she'd ever experienced. It tingled in her fingers and toes, rippled through her body, burned in her blood like jet fuel. It was too much. Too damn much. She collapsed on top of him, convulsing violently through the onslaught of ecstasy.

When she opened her eyes, AJ was grinning up at her. "Say it," he ordered.

She struggled to catch her breath. "Say what?"

"That I was right. That the anticipation was worth it."

As her lower body quivered from the aftershocks of her orgasm, she responded in a grudging tone. "It was worth it."

"Good." The grin never left his face. "Now untie me so we can do that again."

• • •

When AJ entered his office several hours later, he found both his partners waiting there for him. Sprawled in the visitors' chairs by his desk and fiddling on their respective phones, as if they'd been killing time until he showed up.

AJ looked from Reed to Gage, bewildered. "What's up?"

Reed shot him a *duh* look. "Weekly meeting. Remember?"

Crap. He'd forgotten that they'd moved their meeting to Sunday because Gage had taken Friday off to have dinner with his girlfriend and her stepfather.

It also occurred to him that Friday was the night he'd met Brett. Wow. Had it only been two days ago? Christ, they'd had a ludicrous amount of sex in such a short time. It felt like he'd known her for months, years even.

His wrists still bore the damage from their latest round between the sheets—Brett's knots had chafed the hell out of him. AJ hoped his friends wouldn't pay too close attention to his hands. They'd probably be stunned if they knew what kind of kink he'd just participated in.

"Sorry, it slipped my mind," he apologized. "You guys haven't been waiting long, have you?"

"Naah, just ten minutes or so," Gage answered.

Reed's blue eyes twinkled as he pocketed his phone. "So what's her name?"

AJ tensed as two identical smirks appeared on his friends' faces, but he decided to play dumb. "What's whose name?"

Gage snickered. "You're really gonna deny it?"

"We *know* you had a visitor the other night," Reed chimed in. "Jerry told us. Ergo, you're busted."

Damn. AJ should have known Jerry would blab. Sin's employees gossiped more than a group of teenage girls.

"A friend stopped by to say hello. It was no big deal."

"A friend," Reed echoed. "Uh-huh. Suuuuure."

The two men exchanged knowing looks. "He's lying to us," Gage said thoughtfully. "Why do you think that is?"

Reed pursed his lips. "Maybe she's got crazy scars on her face or something?"

"Naah, you know he's not obsessed with looks. Maybe he's in love with her?" Gage suggested.

"Fuck, of course." Reed nodded fervently. "But it's still so new and shiny he doesn't want to share yet. Wants to bask in the glow in private for a while longer. Makes sense."

"Perfect sense," Gage agreed.

AJ flopped down in his chair. "I'm not in love with anyone, and stop talking about me like I'm not in the room." He picked up the inventory sheets on the desktop. "Are we doing this or what?"

To his relief, his friends quit needling him and shuffled their own papers.

He wasn't sure why he'd deflected their questions, but he didn't feel entirely comfortable telling them about Brett. It didn't help that Reed and Gage happened to be dating women who liked to poke their noses into AJ's life. Darcy's nosiness made sense—they'd dated, after all, and AJ knew she desperately wanted him to find the kind of happiness she'd found with Reed. But Gage's girlfriend Skyler was just as dogged in her matchmaking efforts. She'd already tried setting him up with both her roommates, and after he'd shot her down, she'd proceeded to make a list of everyone she'd gone to college with in an attempt to push a love connection on him.

Well, he didn't need help finding dates, and he certainly didn't need Darcy and Skyler latching on to Brett the way they'd latched on to each other. If he introduced them to her, they'd welcome her into the girlfriend fold in a heartbeat. And then, knowing Darcy and Skyler, they'd remain friends with her after she and AJ parted ways, and he'd be forced to see Brett all the time.

Though *forced* was probably the wrong word. Truth was, he was surprised by how much fun he had with the woman. She was strong and outspoken, she made him laugh, she challenged him...

Hell, it was probably a good thing she wasn't looking for a relationship. If circumstances had been different, he'd totally consider turning their temporary arrangement into something more permanent.

But he couldn't. His family situation was too delicate at the moment, and God knew he'd caused his parents enough grief over the years. He'd valiantly tried to be the son they needed him to be, until he'd veered off course and started making one selfish decision after the other. With his mom still recovering from her heart attack, he couldn't afford to be selfish again. His dad would skin him alive if he caused her even a moment's stress.

As amazing as Brett was, his folks would never approve of her. Tattoos and bad-girl clothing aside, she was also younger than him, and focused on her career rather than getting married and popping out babies. His next relationship needed to be with a woman who was ready to settle down, a woman who could help him give his parents the grandchildren they craved.

After the choices he'd made in the past, he at least owed them that.

"He's not listening to us."

Gage's dry voice lured him back to the meeting in progress.

"Shit. Sorry," AJ muttered. "My head's all over the place tonight."

"I wonder why," Reed said mockingly.

"Love does that to a man," Gage piped up.

He stifled a sigh. "So this new supplier," he prompted, shooting them a pointed look. "What's his deal again?"

His friends yet again took pity on him and got back to business. Reed began to outline his plan to start stocking the bar with higher-end liquor, exhibiting a savvy business sense that AJ still found jarring. Growing up, Reed had been a troublemaker with a capital *T*, which was why AJ's parents had forbidden him from spending time with him. But AJ had stood his ground and continued to see the guy. There'd been something very freeing about Reed's lust for life and give-them-hell attitude.

Reed also had a good heart, though, and AJ was proud

of the mature, responsible man his friend had become. These days Reed was working hard to make Sin a success. So was Gage, who'd been equally rough around the edges when AJ first met him at an MMA bout. But since he'd started dating Skyler, Gage was smiling and laughing a lot more these days.

"We also need to hire a few more bouncers," Gage was saying. "We can't get by with one guy manning the door anymore. The line's getting too long, and the bigger crowds are starting to stir up trouble."

"Dude, I'm so not complaining that people are lining up to come here," Reed answered with a grin. "If things keep up this way, we should think about opening another location. Maybe in Portland, or Manhattan."

"You want to leave Boston?" AJ said in surprise.

"Of course not." Reed shrugged. "We could hire a manager to run the place. Just something to think about."

The offhand suggestion reminded AJ of Brett's current situation, and he hoped for her sake that her father gave her a shot to prove herself. It was plain to see that Jimmy Conlon still viewed Brett as a little girl and not the strong woman she was.

The memory of being tied to Brett's bed swiftly flashed to mind, and AJ thanked God that his desk concealed the resulting boner that sprang in his pants.

"His eyes are glazing over again. It's definitely love."

Once more, he was jolted out of his Brett-centered thoughts. "Jeez," he grumbled to Reed. "Give it up already."

Chuckling, his friend stood and tucked his papers under his arm. Gage followed suit, looking equally amused.

"Don't worry, we're going." Reed grinned. "You'll have all the privacy in the world to jerk off to thoughts of your lady love."

AJ flipped them his middle finger, but neither man was fazed. They simply left his office in a burst of laughter and another display of gloating, insufferable smirks.

Chapter Nine

Since the club was closed on Mondays, AJ headed to his parents' place for dinner, armed with a bouquet of white roses for his mom and a bottle of Jack Daniel's for his dad. He knew they'd appreciate the gesture—his mom loved it when he brought her flowers, and his poor dad was so stressed out playing the part of both bread earner and homemaker that he'd definitely welcome a stiff drink.

As always, when he reached the house, dread and reluctance hardened in his chest like a block of cement.

And as always, the first two emotions triggered an even more unwelcome third.

Guilt.

Bone-crushing guilt.

Christ, he was a selfish bastard. He had parents who adored him and a childhood home oozing with warmth. He should have been thrilled to be there tonight, not steeling himself for the visit.

The path to the door was lined with flowers. Normally his mother tended to the front garden, but the men's work gloves and massive rubber boots sitting on the porch told him his dad had taken over gardening duty along with everything else. Which only brought another pang of self-reproach. Since his mother's heart attack, he'd made a point to stop by on the three days of the week that Sin was closed, but that wasn't enough, damn it. A better son would've showed up daily.

He let himself in and kicked off his sneakers. His parents' voices drifted into the hall from the kitchen. From the sound of it, his mother was arguing that she was strong enough to toss a salad, while his dad kept ordering her to sit her butt down.

AJ had to smile. Although his folks' marriage had been plagued with unimaginable heartache, it had endured thanks to hard work and the undeniable love they felt for each other.

"AJ!" Karen Walsh broke out in a delighted smile when he wandered into the room.

His mother rose from her chair by the kitchen table and enveloped him in a big hug. She was a tall woman, and although she'd always been slender, she was considerably frailer since the heart attack. Her hair, a short blond bob streaked with silver, tickled AJ's chin as he gently hugged her back.

"Hey, Mom. How you feeling?"

"Strong as an ox and healthy as a horse," she declared, before glaring at AJ's dad. "It's just too bad your father doesn't believe me."

"Sit down, sweetheart," Tom Walsh said sternly. "If I see you on your feet again, I swear I'll go outside and rip up all the flowers I planted today."

"You wouldn't dare."

"Try me."

AJ watched the ensuing stare-off in amusement. His mom was obsessed with her garden, and sure enough, she was the first to back down. With an exaggerated sigh, she sank back in her chair.

"That's what I thought." Tom gave a satisfied nod, then wiped his hands on a pink dishrag and walked over to clap his son on the back. "Right on time, kiddo. Help me set the table."

They got to setting while Karen chattered on about all the work AJ's father had done in the backyard over the past week. The smells permeating the air were surprisingly appealing, and when Tom served the meatloaf, mashed potatoes, and roasted carrots he'd prepared, AJ couldn't hide his surprise.

"Since when do you make anything that's actually edible?" he asked, grinning at his father.

His mom fielded the question with a sigh. "Since he gave us food poisoning last week."

AJ laughed. "Seriously?"

"Oh yes." Another glower sailed in her husband's direction. "Which is what happens when you don't follow my recipes like I *told* you to."

Tom had the decency to look sheepish. "I learned my lesson, sweetheart. No need to keep lording it over me."

That got a smile out of her. "It *was* incredibly rewarding seeing you huddled over the toilet bowl like that." She picked up her knife and fork, then glanced at AJ. "Don't worry—it's safe to eat this meal. I made sure to taste everything before you got here."

As they settled in to eat dinner, AJ's reluctance faded into a sense of contentment. These were the moments he liked. Listening to his parents' good-natured bickering, seeing the smiles on their faces. And it could be like that all the time, if he just kept playing his part in this Norman Rockwell-esque family sitcom of theirs.

Except the problem with acting? No show stayed on the air forever.

"So when are you going to sell that dance club and come work with me?"

His father's barely veiled disapproval was like a slap to the face across the table. As if on cue, AJ's guard shot up ten feet to shield him from the tense conversation he knew was coming.

"I'm happy where I am," he said carefully. "You know that."

"But you'd be so much happier working with your dad," Karen protested.

Ha. Fat chance. What the hell did he know about selling windows and doors? He'd go insane in a week. No, a *day*.

"The club's doing well," AJ added, ignoring his mother's comment. "Our profits have tripled since we opened our doors."

"Money's all well and good, but don't you want to be in a more respectable line of work?" his father prodded.

Respectable—his least favorite word in the world.

A frustrated groan climbed up his throat, but he choked it down with a mouthful of mashed potatoes. He refused to get into another argument about Sin.

"I'm happy where I am," he repeated.

Fortunately, his parents dropped the subject.

And changed it to an even less desirable one.

"Why hasn't Darcy been coming by lately?" his mother asked.

"I told you. We broke up." Nearly a year ago, he decided not to remind her.

"I know that, sweetie. But you said you two were still friends. I miss seeing her." She made a tsking noise with her tongue. "She's such a sweet girl. Good head on her shoulders." There was a pause. "She'd make a great mother, you know."

AJ waited for it…

"But you're just determined not to give us any grandbabies, aren't you?"

Her tone had a teasing lilt to it, but AJ wasn't fooled.

Coming so close to death had really freaked his mother out, and she was now on his case more than ever to enter a new phase in his life, the one that involved giving her a daughter-in-law to gossip with and a grandchild to dote on.

"I haven't found the right woman yet," he said awkwardly. "But don't worry, I'll let you know the moment I do."

She looked pleased. "Good. Because your father and I aren't getting any younger."

The conversation blessedly shifted again, back to his father's business and all the new clients he'd picked up this past month. After they'd finished eating, AJ helped his dad clear the table, then went to the counter to cut three slices of store-bought apple pie for dessert.

As he handed his parents some pie, he swallowed a lump of despair and tried to maintain a happy-go-lucky demeanor.

But God. It was all so fucking perfect he felt like tearing his hair out. And like clockwork, a familiar itchy sensation pricked at him, the same one that had led him to join Reed's boxing gym when his friend had announced he was going to fight pro. At first, AJ had pretended he was doing it to keep Reed company. He'd been Reed's sparring partner and training buddy, and when Reed had convinced him to fight in a few amateur bouts, he'd acted like he'd needed arm-twisting.

But he'd *wanted* to fight. He'd craved the adrenaline rush, the messed-up sense of peace it brought him.

"Did I tell you I ran into Tamara Howard the other day?" his mother spoke up. "You two went to high school together."

AJ shoveled a massive bite of pie into his mouth in order to delay his response. Tamara had been one of the cheerleaders who'd harassed Brett, and as he remembered that, a vise of possessiveness squeezed his chest.

For some reason, the thought of someone tormenting Brett pissed him off, and he suddenly wished he had the ability to travel back in time so he could stick up for her. But he'd been oblivious back then, sparing no thought to a girl who was three years behind him in school. He'd been too focused on getting a football scholarship.

Another attempt at pleasing his parents, of course. AJ didn't particularly care for football, not the way his father did.

Or the way Joey had.

And bad idea thinking about Joey, because the memory just achieved the same old result: deep rush of guilt and the overpowering need to atone for his sins.

"Yeah…what's she up to?" AJ asked, injecting as much interest in his tone as he could muster.

"She got divorced not too long ago." His mother looked far more delighted than the news warranted. "She has two little girls. She brought her youngest with her to the store—the most adorable baby I've ever seen! Big blue eyes, curly blond hair, cherub cheeks."

"Damn cute baby," his dad agreed.

"She told me to say hello to you. She also gave me her phone number," Karen hedged, a meaningful note ringing in her voice. "I think you should give her a call."

AJ uttered an inward curse.

"I know it might be daunting to date a woman who already has kids, but I think you'd make a wonderful stepfather."

Fuckin' hell. He wasn't married and popping out kids like they wanted, so now they were going to saddle him with a ready-made family?

AJ jammed the rest of his pie in his mouth and chewed as fast as humanly possible, then scraped back his chair and picked up his plate. "Tamara and I didn't have much in common back then," he mumbled. "But sure, maybe I'll give her a call."

Ten minutes later, he left his parents' house with anguish in his heart and the phone number of a woman he didn't care about in his pocket.

"There." Brett dabbed the excess ink from her client's butt. "All done."

"How does it look?" the burly man demanded. "Did you do the shading like I asked?"

"See for yourself." She waited for him to heave his huge body out of her chair, then led him to the full-length mirror against the far wall. She swiped a hand mirror from the counter and held it up behind him, angling it so he had a clear view of his bare ass.

Lou whooped loudly when he saw her handiwork. Two words, done in intricate calligraphy and underlined with barbed wire, just like she'd sketched for him the day before.

Thanks to Brett, the man's chubby, slightly hairy butt officially boasted two words: FUCK YOU.

Yep. The joy of being a tattoo artist. Some of the custom designs Brett had created over the years still boggled her mind, but she'd accepted that the tattoo business was a crazy one. People wanted what they wanted, and she gave it to them without question, judgment, or teasing. If a dude wanted to get the words *fuck you* inked on his ass cheek, who was she to deny him?

Still, she much preferred the clients who showed up with a general idea and then gave her permission to let her creativity soar. Most of the time, they were thrilled by the final design and didn't request a single change. Other times, she had to redraw it dozens of times before the client found what they'd been looking for.

Lou, however, was easy to please. All of his tattoos were various lines of text, and he always tipped handsomely, which she appreciated.

"That'll teach Cindy to tell me I have a fat ass," he crowed. "Now I won't even have to answer her. She'll know exactly what I think of her bullshit criticism when she sees this." Lou slapped his ink-free butt cheek before striding off to get his pants.

"Hey, no, you don't," Brett chided when he tried to get dressed. "You know the drill. Lay back down."

"Aw, come on, I don't need the bandage."

"House rules, bud. We don't let anyone leave without it."

She'd barely finished her sentence when the bell rang in the main room. Crap. Lou was her last client of the night, and it was already five past nine. Since AJ didn't work Mondays, they'd agreed to meet at her place at nine thirty, and she was dying to finish work so she could see him.

Without leaving her station, she gave a hasty shout toward the curtain. "I'll be right with you."

Rob had already left for the night, and though normally she felt comfortable closing up shop alone, her shoulders stiffened when she heard footsteps approaching the curtain.

It opened a slit, and her body relaxed when she found herself staring into a pair of familiar green eyes "Hey. It's me," AJ said softly. "Just didn't want you to think it was a client. I'll wait out here."

He quickly disappeared, but his presence had already sent her pulse galloping. She wasn't sure why he'd come, but she definitely wasn't complaining. If anything, she was even more eager to get rid of Lou now.

She carefully attached the bandage to the man's backside and waited for him to stand up so she could shoot him a stern glare. "Keep it covered for three hours, make sure you use the ointment I gave you last time, and try not to sit down for the first couple days."

"I work in a toll booth, Tinkerbell. How the hell do you expect me not to sit down?"

Tinkerbell. It seemed like every client had their own nickname for her, most of which had to do with her size.

She liked AJ's nickname the best, though. *Angel*. Lord, just thinking about the way he drawled out the word made her tremble.

"Just keep off it when you can," she said with a sigh. "Give it time to heal."

"Yes, ma'am."

Lou slipped into his pants, then reached for his wallet. He'd already paid her upfront for his tattoo, but now he pressed another wad of bills into her hand. "For you," he said gruffly.

"Aw, thanks, Lou."

He ruffled her hair and pulled her in for a bear hug, but there was nothing sexual about the embrace. Lou was well into his forties and treated her like a daughter. And she loved him to pieces. Clients as easygoing as him were hard to come by.

"Pop in next week so we can touch up your arm," she told him as they stepped into the main room.

"Will do." With a big grin and a nod in AJ's direction, Lou left the shop.

The second the door closed behind him, Brett flicked the padlock and shut off the neon OPEN sign. She smiled as she turned back to AJ, but the joy and humor faded when she noticed the expression on his face.

"What's wrong?" she demanded.

Without a word, he stalked over and yanked her toward him for a rough kiss. The tension seemed to seep from his shoulders the moment their lips touched, but when his tongue stole into her mouth with greedy precision, she could taste his need and desperation. Feel the urgency of his body as he pressed it against hers and rotated his hips.

When they broke apart, she was breathless. "Seriously, what's gotten into you?"

"I had a crappy evening," he admitted.

"Aw, that sucks. What happened?"

"Nothing worth talking about." AJ cocked his head. "In fact, I don't feel like talking about anything at all right now. I want you naked."

Brett tried to hide her frustration as he deflected the question by using sex. She was starting to suspect that AJ Walsh harbored a lot of secrets.

And of course, since she couldn't ever spend time with a man without becoming consumed by him, his mysterious nature only made her more desperate to figure him out.

But no. She couldn't fall into that trap again. Her arrangement with AJ worked because it was temporary. As long as she kept viewing him as nothing but a fun sexual partner, she wasn't in danger of losing focus of what mattered.

So rather than force him to tell her what was wrong, she opted to concentrate on what was *right*.

"If you want me naked, then take me home," she said boldly.

"What if I want to take you right here?"

Brett's uneasy gaze drifted to the front window. It was slightly tinted, but not enough to shield them from view of the street if they did the nasty in the main room. Besides, having sex in her family's tattoo parlor was wrong on so many other levels.

When AJ caught sight of where her gaze had traveled, he pursed his lips and said, "Not here then." He took her hand and coaxed her to the back corridor, guiding her behind the thick red curtain that blocked off her workspace.

AJ's mouth curved when he spotted the padded chair in the center of the room.

"Oh yeah, this will work." His voice was low, rippling with desire.

Brett ignored the tight clenching of her thighs. "I'm not going to have sex with you in my place of business," she said primly.

"No? So you're backing out of your end of our agreement?" His expression flickered with challenge.

"How was sex in my shop ever part of the agreement?" she protested.

"I play the part of doting, respectable boyfriend, and in return, you show me a wild time, remember?" He pointed to the tattoo chair. "And *that*, is a wild time."

The image of AJ fucking her right there on the chair flashed to the foreground of her mind, and her entire body shuddered in response.

He chuckled. "Sounds fun, doesn't it?"

God, it did. But…

She hesitated again.

"You locked up for the night, right?"

She nodded.

"And do your brothers or dad usually drop in after hours?"

She slowly shook her head. They never did. Once the shop was closed, they were done for the night.

"Then I don't see a problem."

AJ's hands lowered to his waistband, and her traitorous gaze was drawn to his every movement like a magnet. He slid the belt from its buckle. Undid the button of his trousers. Inched the zipper down.

"C'mon, angel, give me a taste of the wild girl you used to be. I promise you can lock her up again after tonight…" He parted the top of his pants. "At least until the next time I want her to come out."

He was evil. Pure temptation. Sin incarnate.

Brett hadn't been able to say no to him that first night at the club, and evidently that's how it would always be.

"I want to see your cock," she ordered.

A grin lifted his lips. "Good. Because he's dying to see

you."

The moment he released his erection, Brett's mouth went dry with anticipation. God, maybe he was right. Maybe it was healthy to let her inner bad girl out every now and then. What was the harm in throwing caution to the wind and being *bad* again? The shop was closed. Nobody was around.

So why the hell not?

"What do you say we up the stakes?" she said devilishly.

"I thought the only stakes were the ones that involve my cock inside you."

"Where's the fun in that?" When he wiggled his eyebrows, she quickly corrected herself. "Fine, that part is fun, too. But wild? I don't know. And dangerous? Definitely not."

"Huh. So now you're interested in injecting some danger into our sex life?" He sounded amused…and ridiculously intrigued. "How?"

"I propose a wager." She stepped forward and gave his erection an impish squeeze.

He groaned. "What kind of wager?"

"Well…first, you're going to sit your sexy ass down in my chair…"

"Sounds good so far." He thrust into her waiting palm. "Then what?"

"I'm going to climb on top of you."

"Even better…and then?"

"I'm going to screw your brains out."

AJ's cock thickened in her hand, a drop of moisture leaking onto her thumb. "I…" He shivered when she stroked him again. "…really don't see where the wager comes in."

"Oh, didn't I mention?" She smiled broadly. "The first one to come loses."

A laugh rumbled out of his chest. "That sounds more like winning to me."

"You'd think so, huh?" She released him and reached for

her zipper. "But I haven't told you the stakes yet."

"Fine. I'll bite. What happens if I 'lose'?" He used air quotes around the last word, his lips twitching as if he were fighting another laugh.

"I get to tattoo you." Brett wiggled out of her pants and underwear and kicked them away.

AJ's sultry gaze promptly zeroed in on her lower body. His features grew taut with passion for a moment, before his head snapped up as if he'd just realized what she'd said. "Wait, what?"

"I get to tattoo you," she repeated. "You can choose the design and body part, but it's my needle that does it."

"And if you come first?" he countered.

She shrugged. "Then I get another tattoo."

"You already have a million of them. How is that fair?"

He had a point. She mulled it over, then offered a decisive nod. "Fine, if I lose, I get more ink, but *you* get to choose what and where."

Now she had his attention. For half a second, at least, before suspicion once more clouded his face. "No way. I don't take any wagers unless it's an even playing field."

"How is it not?" she demanded.

"Because you're a woman! I could shoot my load just from being *near* you, but chicks don't come at the drop of a hat. You need foreplay and kissing and all that fun stuff. If you sit on my dick without any lead up, you could probably delay your orgasm for hours." He crossed his arms. "No deal."

Argh. AJ and his stupidly valid points.

Brett pondered the dilemma until she found another solution. "You get a handicap then. Ten minutes of oral sex."

"Ha. I won't last ten *seconds* if you put your mouth on my—"

"For me," she clarified. "Ten minutes of oral sex for *me*."

That shut him up, bringing the thoughtful glint back to

his eyes.

"Think about it," she said in her most tempting tone. "You'll have ten whole minutes to tease me and torture me and get me close. And we both know how good you are at doing that."

A sigh escaped as she realized she'd effectively stacked the odds against her. AJ knew it too as he splayed his palm on her belly and slowly dragged it over her mound. His eyes twinkled when he felt the evidence of her arousal.

Brett ignored the ripples of pleasure that danced through her. "So? Deal or no deal?" she challenged.

He chuckled. "Deal. *Definitely* deal."

She moaned when he slipped one finger inside her.

"I can't wait to pick your new tat, baby." He ground the heel of his hand over her clit. "How do you feel about portraits? More specifically—a portrait of me giving two thumbs up?" He tickled the top of her mound. "Right here."

His cockiness only fueled Brett's competitive spirit. Arching one brow, she cupped his blond head with both hands and pushed him down to his knees. "Bring it, *baby*. Bring it."

Chapter Ten

"He's good for you."

Brett looked up from her sketchpad to find her brother's face peering down at her. She hadn't even heard him approach, and yet there he was, tattooed forearms resting on the counter as he eyed her in amusement.

"Who's good for me?" she said absently, her pencil still moving over the pad.

"AJ. Duh."

She hoped her brother didn't notice the way her shoulders had stiffened in discomfort. "Is he?"

"Absolutely. We all love him, by the way. Dude fits right in."

Brett couldn't even contradict him. AJ *did* fit right in. It had been more than a week since she'd introduced him to her family, and he'd already hung out with them several times since the barbecue. The night before, she and AJ had gone out for drinks with her brothers, which had turned a tad chaotic when Jordan and his on-again/off-again girlfriend Jessica had gotten into a screaming match.

Brett hated the woman, and to this day, she still had no clue what her brother saw in such a high-maintenance, manipulative bi-otch. But she'd been impressed by AJ's composure during the fight. He hadn't cut and run like she'd expected, and once the squabbling couple had left the pub, she and AJ ended up having a great time with Rob and Mike, whose shrilly impressions of Jessica were spot-on.

"Seriously, every time I see you, you've got a big goofy smile on your face. I'd totally bust your balls about it if it weren't so frickin' cute." Rob was positively beaming at her. "My little sister is in love. I'm so proud."

She rolled her eyes. "I'm not in love. AJ and I are just casual."

Rob didn't look convinced. "If you say so." He shrugged. "Either way, it's nice to see you happy for a change. I'm glad you kicked that fucker Troy to the curb."

"Don't remind me." Her chest tightened at the mention of her ex. "God. I can't believe he turned out to be such a jerk."

"Forget about him. You're with a guy that makes you happy now, and that's all the matters."

Brett faltered as the words sank in. She supposed she *was* happy. What she and AJ had might be casual, but she was perfectly content with that.

Though she had been making an effort to keep a slight distance from him. Not reveal too much, not push him too hard. She and relationships were like a bottle of alcohol and a loaded gun—not a great combo. When she was in love, she forgot about the rest of the world, so eager to please her partner that they ended up walking all over her.

Fortunately, she and AJ had fallen into a routine she could live with. He came over to her place, they had sex, hung out. Sure, they'd been making a point to see her family so Brett could push her responsibility agenda, but there were no heart-to-hearts, no promises, no longing glances.

And she didn't mind at all.

Liar. You mind.

Nope, she wasn't listening to the yearning voice in her head. She and AJ had a good thing going. She didn't want a relationship. He didn't want a relationship.

Win win.

And an extra win for the explosive sex.

"So did he pick a design yet?"

Of course, Rob just *had* to remind her of the one thing she *wasn't* winning at.

Brett scowled at her brother. "No, he hasn't. And don't you dare remind me of it."

Rob chortled. "I still can't believe you thought it was a good idea to bet on a chess match. You *suck* at chess."

Yeah, and apparently she sucked at not orgasming, too. But her family didn't know about *that*. Last night, when AJ had nonchalantly revealed that she'd lost a bet and thus given him the power to choose her next tattoo, Brett had scrambled to think of a plausible, nonsexual bet they could have made. Chess was the first thing that came to mind, and now she was kicking herself for coming up with such a harebrained lie.

Damn AJ and his magic cock. She couldn't even look at her tattoo chair anymore without remembering how quickly she'd come in his lap last week.

"I spoke to Dad, by the way."

Rob's offhand comment purged all the dirty thoughts from her head. "About what?" She didn't bother masking her excitement.

"You know, about how good you're doing, what a great help you've been around the shop, how smart and wonderful and brilliant you are, yada, yada, yada."

"Did he say anything about the new Conlon Ink location?" She held her breath as she awaited his reply.

"Nothing official," Rob admitted. "But if it helps, I was over at the house when Dad got a phone call from that artist he was talking to. The guy who works at Razor's?"

Brett bristled with displeasure. She'd known her dad was interviewing potential candidates to run the north end parlor, but hearing Rob confirm it ticked her off. The ideal candidate was staring them all in the face, damn it.

Her.

"He canceled the interview," Rob said lightly.

Her breath came out in an abrupt whoosh. "Really?"

"Yup. Mind you, he hasn't said one way or the other if he's going to give you a shot, but this is a good sign, right?"

No, it was a *fabulous* sign.

Brett dove off the chair and threw her arms around her brother. "Oh my God. I don't believe it. He's totally going to let me manage the shop!"

"Possibly." Rob's voice went gentle. "But don't put the cart before the horse just yet." He hesitated. "Maybe I shouldn't have said anything."

"No, I'm glad you did. Now I'm going to work even harder, until he has no choice but to admit that I'm the best person for the—"

A loud *ding* interrupted her. She swung her head in the direction of the door—then froze.

Brett's jaw fell open as her ex-boyfriend entered the tattoo parlor.

What. The. Hell.

"Hey," Troy said cautiously.

All she could do was gape at him. Holy shit. He really had the nerve to waltz in here after everything he'd put her through? The mere sight of him made Brett want to clock him.

And to add insult to injury, the bastard actually looked *good*. Like, really, really good. A black T-shirt hugged his chest and showed off the intricate tattoos on each of his biceps, and he'd cut his hair and shaved his goatee since she'd last seen him. Goddamn him. He didn't deserve to be this handsome.

Brett still remembered the way he'd drawn her in last year with those killer dimples and reckless personality. But he'd been *too* reckless. Troy had no off button when it came to partying. For him, one beer was never enough—he had to have ten. Not only that, but he was a frickin' sponge. He took and took and took and never once gave anything in return. Whether it was a dinner she'd prepared for him, a free tattoo she'd spotted him, or a ride home when he was too plastered to drive, the jerk had never expressed an ounce of gratitude or appreciation. Not even once.

"What are you doing here?" Brett demanded when she finally found her voice.

Troy came to the counter as if he were approaching a feral lion. "Can we talk in private?" His blue-eyed gaze darted to Rob, whose expression was frigid enough to freeze the Pacific.

Shit. Brett suddenly remembered that Rob had been with her the morning after her trip to the drunk tank. He'd played the part of bodyguard when Troy came over to pick up some things he'd left at her apartment, and the confrontation between the two men hadn't been pretty, to say the least.

"No, we can't," she said coldly. "What do you want, Troy?"

"You're really going to make me do this in front of *him*?" he demanded in a plaintive voice.

"Do what? There's no reason for you to be here." She crossed her arms, mostly so she wouldn't act on the urge to smack him in the face. "In fact, I'd like you to leave."

"I miss you," Troy mumbled.

Rob snorted.

"I do," he insisted. "I miss you so much. These past six months without you have been pure torture, baby."

"Don't you dare call me that! And forgive me if I don't believe a word you say."

His expression took on a pleading light. "I mean it. You're all I can think about."

"Wow. Really? Did you also think about me when you *cheated* on me?"

"I…" His Adam's apple twitched as he swallowed. "I already apologized for that. I was drunk, okay? I didn't know—"

"What you were doing?" she finished. "Yeah, I'm sure you were totally incapacitated when you unzipped your pants and stuck it in some other girl." She planted both palms on the countertop, needing to ground herself, fighting the increasing urge to hit him.

She'd found out about the cheating after they'd broken up, and the knowledge was as humiliating now as it had been then.

And having her big brother hear how she'd been played for a fool only intensified the embarrassment scorching her cheeks.

"You need to go," she muttered. "We're not together anymore. I don't want you in my life."

"Brett, please—"

Rob cut in with a death glare. "You heard my sister, asswipe. Get lost."

Silence crashed over the room. Her ex-boyfriend looked from her to Rob, then down at his feet. Several seconds ticked by before he spoke again.

"I'm not drinking anymore, Brett. I cleaned up my act, went to rehab, got my shit together. I just want another chance to prove to you that I'm the man you fell in love with."

"Not interested," she retorted.

Unhappiness clouded his face. "If you change your mind—"

"I won't."

"You can reach me at the shop. I don't have my cell

anymore."

Yeah, because he never paid his damn bills.

"I'm working on getting a new one, though," he said hastily, as if reading her mind. "Please. Just give me another chance."

Brett didn't answer. Simply cocked her head at the door and transmitted a silent *get the hell out*.

"I'll be waiting for your call," Troy said sadly, edging away from the counter.

"Then you'll be waiting a long time," Rob told his retreating frame.

A moment later, Troy was gone.

Far too mortified and ashamed to meet her brother's eyes, Brett inhaled a ragged breath and picked up her sketchbook with trembling fingers. "I need to finish this drawing," she mumbled.

A warm hand rested on her shoulder, making her jump. "Are you okay?"

"I'm fine." Another deep inhalation, and she was finally able to lift her head. "Thanks for sticking up for me, but you didn't have to. I can handle Troy."

"I know, but you shouldn't have to. That prick needs to learn that he's no longer part of your life. In fact, someone ought to send him a message, just so he's clear on that."

Alarm skittered up her spine when she glimpsed the severe look on her brother's face. "No. Don't you dare rustle up Mike and Jordan and go after him. Troy knows where I stand. He won't come back."

Rob's jaw tightened. "Do you truly believe that?"

"Yes. But it doesn't matter what I believe. I don't need or appreciate your interference. I'm a big girl, Rob. I can take care of myself." She exhaled in a rush. "Please. Promise me you'll back off."

A beat of hesitation, and then he sighed. "Fine. I won't

send a message."

Relief swept over her. "Thank you."

"But"—Rob was quick to voice a caveat—"if he comes around again, I can't make the same promise."

"He won't," she said firmly.

But deep down, she wasn't so sure.

Troy's unexpected visit had left Brett so shaken up she decided to cancel on AJ that night, but when she got home after work, she was surprised to find his Jeep already parked at the meter.

Crap. He was early.

She parked a few spaces ahead of him, then made sure her parking permit was visible on the dash. Her apartment didn't have a driveway or garage, which meant she had no choice but to leave her car on the street. She'd used to worry that it might get stolen, but she'd learned pretty fast that nobody wanted to steal her beat-up hatchback. Fixing it up would no doubt cost more money than anyone could make selling it.

Her boots connected with the sidewalk at the same time AJ strode toward her. Since the club was closed, he wasn't wearing his all-black bartender clothes but his preppy getup—jeans, a white T-shirt, and sneakers on his feet.

In her black leather pants, bloodred tank top and high-heeled boots, Brett knew she and AJ looked like the last two people who'd ever get together, yet when his lips touched hers in a kiss hello, their mouths fit together perfectly.

"I was going to call you to cancel," she admitted when they'd pulled back.

He frowned. "What's wrong?"

"Nothing major or anything. I just had a crappy day, and I'm not really in the mood for sexy times." She paused. "You can go if you want."

He looked surprised. "Why would I go? Do you want me to?"

Brett wrinkled her forehead. "Well, no, but…you know, this was supposed to be about sex." She fidgeted with her hands. "If there's no sex tonight, there's no reason for you to be here."

"Sure there is. We can still hang out." It was his turn to shift in discomfort. "Unless you don't want to…?"

Brett bit her lip, torn. She wouldn't mind the company, but she hadn't been kidding about not being in the mood. It seemed impossible, considering that all AJ had to do was *look* at her and her panties melted off, but her mind was too muddled at the moment. Seeing Troy had reminded her of a chapter in her life she was desperate to forget, and not even AJ could distract her from that tonight.

Times like these, only some trashy television and a carton of ice cream did the trick.

"Have you eaten?" she asked him.

He nodded. "I had dinner at my folks' house."

"Good, because there's nothing in my fridge, so I wouldn't have been able to feed you." Ugh, which also meant no ice cream. Damn it. "I desperately need to get some groceries."

"Why don't we do that now?"

The suggestion threw her for a loop. "You want to go grocery shopping together?"

"Why not? We might as well stock up your fridge, seeing as you're not in the mood…"

The humor in his eyes made it clear he was just teasing her. He genuinely seemed okay that she'd taken sex off the table, and she appreciated that he wasn't trying to coax her into getting naked.

"Okay," she said with a shrug. "Let's do it then."

"I'll drive," he replied, taking her hand and leading her to his Jeep. "Where do you want to go?"

The Kims' store was already closed for the night, so she directed him to the twenty-four-hour grocery mart three blocks away. Five minutes later, they were pushing a squeaky cart through the air-conditioned aisles.

Talk about surreal.

Brett noticed several shoppers sneaking peeks at her arms as she passed by. It was a common occurrence—people always stared at her tattoos, and she didn't mind it, especially since most of the time it was out of admiration. Every now and then, though, the attention stemmed from disapproval and judgment.

Case in point—the woman they encountered in the cereal aisle.

Middle-aged and harried-looking, the blonde was pushing an overloaded cart while two little girls trailed after her, bouncing excitedly on their tiny pink sneakers.

"Pretty!" one of the girls exclaimed, pointing to the cluster of roses around Brett's wrist.

The child's mother was quick to correct her. "Not pretty," she said in a stern voice. "It's mutilation, sweetie." With a pointed look, she added, "And very inappropriate."

As inappropriate as taking two small children grocery shopping at nine thirty on a school night? Brett was tempted to snipe back.

"What's mootilation?" the other girl asked.

The woman didn't even look Brett's way as she and her daughters disappeared around the corner. Brett couldn't hear her response to the children, but she didn't need to be a genius to figure out what it would be. Something scathing, no doubt.

"Ignore that," AJ murmured to her.

She offered a wry look before scanning the wall of cereal boxes in search of the one she wanted. "Don't worry. I'm used to those types of reactions. You're the one I feel bad for. You poor thing, associating with someone so mutilated and inappropriate."

His soft chuckle heated the back of her neck. "I happen to find your mutilated body very sexy."

"Aw, thank you." She spotted her favorite cereal and leaned up on her tiptoes, but she was too short to reach the top shelf.

AJ snickered and took pity on her, coming up beside her to grab the box of Corn Pops. His arm brushed hers, bare skin grazing bare skin, and she broke out in goose bumps. Jeez. There'd been nothing sexual about the contact, yet her entire body tingled like crazy.

Maybe she was in the mood, after all.

But since they were already at the grocery store, she forced herself to banish the temptation to abandon the cart and drag him home.

"Seriously, though, how many other girls covered in tats have you gone out with?" she asked curiously.

"Not many," he confessed.

"None, I bet."

"Fine. None."

"Have any of your girlfriends been bat-shit crazy?"

"No, I can't say they have. Why? Do I need to worry about any bat-shit crazy exes of yours tracking me down and killing me?"

"Probably not." She paused in the next aisle, swiping a jar of olives from the shelf and carefully placing it in the cart.

"Probably?" AJ echoed. "That doesn't sound promising at all."

"I already told you, I've dated some jerks in the past." Brett hesitated, then decided she might as well be completely honest with him. "One of them showed up at the tattoo parlor today."

"Yeah?"

"This guy Troy. He strolled right in and announced that

he wants me back."

AJ's broad shoulders stiffened, but it was difficult to interpret the response. Was he jealous? Angry on her behalf? Despite his rigid body language, his shuttered expression revealed nothing.

"I see," AJ said slowly. "And do you want him back?"

"Hell no." She spoke with unwavering conviction. "But seeing him was kind of…I don't know…depressing, I guess? It reminded me of all the time I invested in the relationship. All the time I wasted."

"There's no such thing as a waste of time." AJ shrugged. "The way I see it, everything we do, every decision we make, good or bad, is just a learning opportunity."

"Yeah, well, I learned never to trust men with dimples."

He grinned at her, and the dimple in his chin popped out as if on cue. "Aw. You don't trust me, angel?"

"Not in the slightest," she said cheerfully. "You're an evil man who does evil things to my body."

"Ha. You like it. Scratch that—you *love* it." His teasing expression shifted back to curiosity. "So what kind of horrendous things did this Troy do to you?"

"At the beginning? Nothing. I was head over heels in love with him. He was fun and adventurous and made me laugh. We had a ton in common—he's a tattoo artist, too. A ridiculously talented one." She frowned. "At least when he bothers to show up for work."

"A bum, huh?" AJ said as they headed down the next aisle.

"Naah, just a guy who likes to have a good time." Sighing, she tossed two packages of linguine into the cart. "He wasn't the greatest influence on me. If he wanted to close the bar on a Monday night, I'd be right there with him. If he felt like blowing off work for a couple of days and driving up to Maine for a spontaneous beach trip, I was like, sign me up." Another breath slipped out, this one heavy with regret. "When I'm in a relationship, I give it everything I have. I work so hard to make the other person happy."

"That's not necessarily a bad thing."

"It is when you're the one making all the compromises." She stopped in the frozen-food aisle. "And it's even worse when you do it against your better judgment. I mean, I *knew* I shouldn't have been out at the bar when I had to be up early the next morning, but I couldn't say no to Troy. He was addictive."

AJ sidled up to her as she started piling cartons of ice cream into the cart. "So how did it end?"

She was grateful for the cold air shivering out of the freezer, because her cheeks had gone hot with embarrassment. "We were at a pub, and Troy picked a fight with some guy who wouldn't give up the pool table. It escalated real fast, and the owner called the cops. They ended up taking me in, too."

"Shit," AJ murmured.

Brett pretended to focus on a shelf of frozen veggies so she wouldn't have to look at him. "My dad had to bail me out." She nearly choked on the shame lining her throat. "It was *mortifying*. That's when I realized I couldn't have someone like Troy in my life. It didn't matter how much fun we had together. He wasn't good for me. So I ended it. And then, a few weeks later, I found out from a friend that he'd been cheating on me the entire time we were together."

AJ whistled under his breath. "Sounds like a real prince. And he came by to see you today?"

"Yep."

"Man. I can see why you're in a bad mood."

"More like a sad mood." She turned away from the freezer and examined the cart. She'd gotten everything she'd needed, and as she and AJ headed for the checkout line, she glanced over with a dry look. "I'm betting there aren't any stories like that in *your* dating history."

"No," he confessed. "The girls I've dated have been pretty wholesome. You know, the type you can bring home to mom."

His words evoked a spark of hurt, even though she knew it wasn't a specific dig at her. Yes, he'd met *her* family, but that was because they were putting on a show for them. There was no reason for Brett to meet *his* parents.

Except...she suspected that even if they had an official relationship, he still wouldn't take her to meet them. She was the furthest thing from wholesome. Hell, she'd literally chased someone out of a grocery aisle five minutes ago.

"What are your parents like?" She halted five feet from the line so they were out of earshot of the other customers.

Uneasiness creased his features, the way it always seemed to do when he mentioned his family. He'd told her about his brother dying, but other than that, she had no idea what his family life was like.

"They're...nice," he said vaguely. "But very traditional about some things."

"Like what?"

"You know, marriage, kids, white picket fences. They've been married for forty years, and honestly? They really do have the perfect relationship. They hardly ever fight, they tell each other everything, they're madly in love." He paused, a faraway light in his eyes. "They want the same thing for me. They want me to be smart and successful, marry the perfect woman, have perfect children."

Brett carefully edged in. "Like I said last week, perfection doesn't exist."

"Tell that to them." No mistaking the bitterness hardening his features.

And the...guilt?

God, sometimes it was impossible to read this man.

"But what about what you want?" she pointed out. "I mean, it's nice that they want all these things for you, but do *you* want to get married and have kids?"

"Sure. One day." His jaw tensed, and then he corrected himself. "No, I want it now."

Brett raised her eyebrows. "Really?"

With a pained expression, he curled his hands over the metal edge of the cart. "Really. That's what I'm looking for in my next relationship—someone who's ready to settle down."

The sting returned, which only added to her confusion. The reminder that she wasn't in a relationship with AJ troubled her more than she wanted to admit, but not as much as the conflicting emotions flashing on his face. He was deeply upset, yet she couldn't figure out why.

And his next revelation just made her head spin harder.

"Look, I owe it to them, okay?"

Brett didn't get a chance to respond. He was already gone, steering the cart toward the line. The elderly woman ahead of them had just paid for her groceries, which meant they were next in line, leaving Brett no opportunity to question him.

She swallowed her distress and impatience as they rang the groceries through, but the second they stepped outside, she couldn't hold back any longer.

"What do you mean, you *owe* it to them?"

AJ didn't meet her eyes as he unlocked the Jeep. A second later, he was loading the bags in the back, acting like she wasn't even there.

But Brett refused to let it go.

"What did you mean by that?" she demanded, scrambling into the passenger's seat as AJ started the car. "Why exactly do you think you owe your parents something?"

A groove appeared in his forehead. Slowly, he glanced over, acknowledging her presence.

"Why?" she pressed.

His voice came out in an angry rush. "Because I'm the reason their son died."

Chapter Eleven

Christ. The last thing AJ wanted to do was bare his soul in the parking lot of a Fresh Mart, but once the confession flew out, he couldn't take it back.

In the passenger seat, Brett was staring at him with wide eyes. Her jaw had fallen open, and he saw her swallowing repeatedly as she tried to make sense of what he'd said.

When she spoke, her voice was low and gentle. "Your brother Joey?"

AJ nodded. Took a breath. It was difficult, though, when agony had slashed his insides to pieces. "He died because of me."

Brett reached across the center console and squeezed his hand. "Tell me what happened."

Fuck. No. He didn't want to relive that night. He'd never told anyone about it before. Reed, Gage, Darcy...all they knew was that he'd had an older brother who'd died before the Walshes had moved to Boston, but that was it. Nobody knew the whole story.

Nobody knew the truth.

"Tell me," Brett repeated.

Her fingers laced through his, grounding him to her, easing the massive load of guilt crushing his chest.

"My family used to live in Vermont." He winced at the crack in his voice. "We had a huge property outside of Burlington, pretty much surrounded by forest."

He halted.

Brett waited.

"I was a total brat when I was a kid," he said gruffly. "I argued with my parents all the time, broke all their rules."

He stopped again.

She waited.

"And I told you what Joey was like, right?"

"Perfect," she murmured.

AJ's heart clenched. "I know you don't believe me, but he was. He was the perfect son, and I was the hell-raiser. I just wanted to run around in the woods and explore and do whatever the hell I wanted."

"That's what most kids are like," she pointed out.

"Maybe. But I took it too far." His hands clenched into fists, and he quickly had to loosen them before he crushed Brett's fingers. "I don't even remember what I was pissed off about, but one day I just flipped out about something my parents had done, some rule they'd probably tried to make me follow, so I ran away." He laughed harshly. "I decided I wasn't going to let them boss me around anymore. I was going to live in the woods and hunt for food and catch fish and live off the land."

He went quiet, for so long that Brett didn't wait this time.

"What happened?" she urged.

"I was gone for hours. Built myself a little fort out of branches, stuffed myself with candy I'd stolen from the house. I was living the dream." Bile rose in his throat and seared his windpipe. "And while I was having the time of my life, the whole neighborhood was combing the woods looking for me. It was late by then, two, three in the morning, and I'd been missing for more than fourteen hours."

"Whoa. Your parents must have been freaking out."

"They were in a panic. So was Joey." AJ bit the inside of his cheek, so hard he tasted blood in his mouth. "I might have hated my parents, but I loved Joey. He was a damn good brother. Didn't matter that he was eight years older than me. He treated me like I was his best friend. He took me camping, played catch with me, taught me how to fish."

"He was looking for you that night?"

AJ clamped his lips together, trying to collect his rapidly crumbling composure. But he forced himself to go on. "He led the search party. It was dark out, and there were dozens of people traipsing around in the forest—because of me. I was the reason they were out there."

"AJ…what happened to Joey?"

His throat closed up. Christ, he couldn't breathe. His lungs had seized up.

Brett touched his cheek, her dark eyes shining with warmth and assurance. "Hey, it's okay. You don't have to keep going if you don't want to. It's okay."

She'd given him an out. He didn't have to keep talking. Didn't have to think about the horror slashing his father's face when AJ had found him on that rocky slope. The vicious bolt of betrayal that had struck AJ's chest when he'd met his father's eyes.

"I heard the shouts," he choked out. "That's what made me come out of my hiding spot. People were screaming, but it wasn't my name they were screaming anymore." His eyelids stung so badly his vision became a foggy blur. "He tripped, Brett. He tripped, fell down a hill, and broke his neck."

Her sharp gasp echoed through the Jeep. "Oh my God. I'm so sorry."

She was touching his face now, cupping his cheeks, brushing her thumbs over the sheen of moisture leaking from his eyes. AJ sagged toward her, his forehead resting against hers as the old wounds he'd opened wreaked havoc on his body.

"He was out there that night looking for me, and he died because of me." His heart beat faster, a frantic rhythm against his rib cage. "They blamed me, too."

"Your parents?" she whispered.

His head dropped on her shoulder, and the familiar scent of her skin succeeded in clearing his head. He looked up and nodded. "They never said it out loud, but I knew they blamed me. Hell, I blamed myself. I got their favorite son killed. I took away their pride and joy."

"I'm sure it must have felt that way, but from what you've told me, your parents don't seem like malicious people," she said quietly. "I'm sure they saw the situation for what it was—a tragic accident."

"All they saw was me," he corrected. "The son whose reckless actions killed Joey. And they had every right. I was selfish. I didn't care about consequences. I just did whatever the hell I wanted, and as a result, my big brother died." Self-loathing trickled down his spine in steady drops. "We left Vermont six months after the funeral. My parents couldn't stand living in the house where Joey had grown up, so we moved to Boston, started over, and that's when I made a decision. No, a promise."

"A promise to what?"

"To be better, damn it. To be *good*."

• • •

As Brett stared into AJ's anguished green eyes, all the puzzle pieces slipped into place. God, the reason she hadn't been able to pin down exactly who he was…it was because he was trying to be someone else.

The revelation brought a deep ache to her heart. The All-American good-guy hero image he tried to project was a direct result of his brother's death. AJ had stepped up to take his perfect brother's place, and in the process, he'd hidden his true self from the people in his life.

But not from her. Yes, she'd seen his gentleman side. She'd seen the easygoing, playful AJ. But she'd also glimpsed the sides he didn't show the rest of the world. The bossy alpha male. The fighter. The business owner. The wild man who craved excitement and met any challenge.

"You *are* good," she said fiercely. "And if your parents don't see that, then screw them."

But even as she said the words, she realized that the issue wasn't with AJ's parents. *He* didn't see himself as worthy, and it was a flawed belief that had formed the night his brother died.

"Easier said than done," AJ said in a tired voice. "I can't just write my folks off. They're good people, and I love them. It's not their fault that I keep screwing up."

"How have you screwed up?" she challenged.

In a monotone voice, he listed off a long list of "faults." "I didn't play professional ball like my dad wanted. I got into MMA fighting instead of going to college. I opened a nightclub instead of working for his company. I broke up with Darcy, who they considered the perfect woman."

He'd mentioned Darcy before, just in passing, but this latest reference made Brett's shoulders stiffen. Perfect woman, huh?

Did it make her an awful person that she now officially *hated* AJ's ex-girlfriend?

"I keep straying off the path I set for myself and disappointing them," AJ said. "But I can't screw up anymore.

My mom's health isn't the greatest these days. She had a heart attack a while back, almost died. She needs grandchildren, a daughter-in-law to talk to…"

"What about what you need?" Brett countered.

His body tensed with visible frustration. "Who says my needs and theirs are mutually exclusive?"

Brett, for one, but she kept her opinion to herself. AJ was agitated enough as it was, and she didn't want to push him any harder than she already had. But she saw right through his feeble declaration.

He'd said so himself—he only dated nice, "wholesome" girls. But after almost two weeks with the guy, Brett knew his tastes ran toward not so nice. He was wild and rough and absolutely *spectacular* when he allowed himself to let go.

It suddenly dawned on her that she and AJ weren't all that different. Both trying to please their families, both fighting their impulsive urges and hiding bits and pieces of themselves from the people they loved.

"C'mon," he said gruffly. "We should head back before all that ice cream you bought starts to melt."

They drove back to her apartment in silence, but Brett wasn't concerned with the lack of conversation. They'd done a lot of talking just now, and her brain was still struggling to work through all the data AJ had fed into it.

AJ the gentleman made an appearance when they reached her place. He carried all the bags upstairs, despite her protests that she could handle at least *one*. But he was adamant, stepping aside only so she could unlock the door, then marching into her kitchen to help her put away the groceries.

"So chivalrous," she teased.

"It's the least I can do after dumping my whole life story on you."

Brett closed the cupboard and walked over to him, resting

her palms on his chest. "Hey, you didn't dump anything. I *wanted* to hear it."

He hesitated. "I've never told anyone about how Joey died."

The confession brought a strange rush of warmth to her chest. "I'm glad you told me."

He lifted his hand and tucked a strand of hair behind her ear. "Can I…uh…how would you feel if I crashed here tonight?"

She blinked in surprise. "You want to sleep over?"

He nodded.

A quick glance at the clock over the fridge revealed that it was already past ten. She had to wake up early for a seven-o'clock appointment because her client couldn't come any other time. And besides…

"Don't worry, I'm not in the mood either," he said as if reading her mind. "And you can kick me out tomorrow morning whenever you have to go."

"I know. It just feels weird for you to stay over when, um, you know, when we won't be doing sexy stuff."

"You make it sound like I'm a sex-starved maniac," he grumbled.

She stared at him.

"Fine, you do bring out that side of me," he conceded. "But I'm a big boy. I'm perfectly capable of keeping my pants zipped and just hanging out with you." He sounded pensive. "What would you be doing right now if I wasn't here?"

She instantly clammed up. "Nothing."

"Liar." He grasped her chin, tugging it upward so she was forced to look at him. "Come on, spill. I promise not to tell."

Heat bloomed in her cheeks. "Fine. If you weren't here, I'd bust open a carton of chocolate mocha mousse and watch a few episodes of the *Vampire Diaries*."

AJ gawked at her. "You're joking."

"Nope." He looked so horrified she couldn't help but laugh. "It's one of my guilty pleasures. Seriously, I'm addicted to trashy teenager shows. I watch them every night before bed."

"Wow. You really don't strike me as the type."

She wagged her finger at him. "Hey, I thought we discussed the whole judging-a-book-by-its-cover thing. You're not nice, and I watch cheesy television shows. Deal with it."

"Yes, ma'am." He sighed heavily. "Fine, I guess I'm in. But you're gonna have to catch me up because I've never seen an episode of that show in my life."

Brett beamed at him. "Oh my God. You don't know what you're missing." Her earlier reluctance vanished as she took his hand and dragged him toward the living room. "Okay, so there's a town full of vampires, and this girl—Elena—is torn between two vampire brothers. They're both smoking hot, but one of them is kind of a dick. He's the one I'm rooting for, though. Trust me, he's *way* more interesting than the other one…"

AJ—God bless his sexy soul—didn't utter a single disparaging remark while she chattered on about the show, and as they cuddled together on the couch, it occurred to her that they'd reached a turning point tonight.

Only she had no idea what it was, or where it would lead them.

Chapter Twelve

"So…what are you wearing?" AJ drawled the second Brett picked up the phone.

Her laughter danced over the line and tickled his ear. "A very skimpy dress, actually. You'd like it. It barely covers my thighs."

The words sent a spike of lust straight to his cock. As his mind conjured up the image of her firm, creamy thighs, he wished she were there right now so he could yank her dress up and bury his face between her legs.

Yup. After two and a half weeks, his overwhelming desire for the woman still hadn't dwindled. If anything, he just desired her *more*.

But in a few days, Brett's father would make his decision about who'd be running the new studio, which meant AJ wouldn't have to pretend to be Brett's upstanding, responsible boyfriend anymore. The thought disturbed him more than it should, and a part of him didn't want their time together to end yet. It was an idea he'd been toying with ever since the night at the grocery store. He'd shown Brett the ugliest part of himself when he'd confessed to the selfish act that had gotten his brother killed—and she hadn't shied away from him.

Brett's reaction hadn't eliminated the guilt—he doubted that would ever go away—but she'd made him feel...whole. For the first time in his life, he'd experienced an actual sense of belonging.

"AJ? You there?"

He snapped out of his thoughts, realizing he'd lapsed into dead air. "Are you on your way to the bar?" he asked. It was Jordan's birthday, so he knew Brett was meeting up with her brothers to celebrate.

"Yep. I wanted to have a couple drinks tonight, so I'm walking over there."

"Crap. I was hoping you hadn't left yet. I decided to join you after all."

"Really?" She sounded delighted. "I thought you were working."

"I was supposed to, but one of my barbacks asked for extra hours. There's no reason for me to stick around if he's here."

"Then you definitely have to come by. Jessica's going to be there, and I could use the moral support. One of these days I'm going to lose my temper and break her nose, you know."

AJ cringed at the memory of Jordan's shrieky girlfriend. Christ, he had no idea what Brett's brother saw in the woman. Actually, scratch that. He knew *exactly* what Jordan saw—a gorgeous blonde with endless legs and a rack liable to make men drool.

AJ had learned a long time ago that looks didn't make the woman, but unfortunately, he couldn't exactly say anything to Brett's brother about it. Jordan had readily admitted to being unable to "quit" the girl, and there wasn't much anyone could do to change that.

"I'll be there within the hour," AJ told her. "Which pub

is it again?"

"The one on Cambridge. Donaghy's—"

A swell of music drowned out Brett's voice as the office door swung open. When Reed appeared in the doorway, AJ held up his hand, signaling for his friend to wait.

"I'll be there soon," he murmured into the phone, then hung up abruptly.

Propping one hip against the doorframe, Reed cast him a meaningful look. "The girlfriend, huh?"

"I already told you, I don't have a girlfriend," he said irritably.

In fact, he'd gone to great lengths to keep his friends in the dark about Brett. He hadn't asked her to come to the club since that first night, and they spent all their time at her apartment in Allston, which meant there was no chance of running into Reed or Gage, who both lived in Southie. It wasn't that he was ashamed of her—he'd willingly parade her all over the damn city…if they were actually dating.

But they weren't, and he had no desire to advertise their fling status to his friends, who'd only harass him like crazy if they knew.

"Fine, let's say you're not seeing anyone," Reed said as he strode inside and closed the door behind him. "Then why don't you explain what's going on with you? You haven't been yourself lately."

AJ was taken aback by the genuine concern in Reed's blue eyes. He was about to reassure his friend, but found himself tamping the urge. He was always the one offering reassurances, the one who smoothed out whatever issues arose. Hell, it was because of *him* that Reed and Darcy were even together. If AJ hadn't stepped in and smacked some sense into them last year, they'd still be wallowing in misery, too blind to see what a good thing they had.

Well, he wasn't in the mood to take on the make-everyone-else-feel-better role tonight.

"I'm exactly who I've always been," he replied with a shrug.

Reed stood in front of the desk, crossing his muscular arms. "No, you're not. I barely see you anymore, and we work in the same damn place! You're constantly ducking out to go see your mysterious non-girlfriend, you hardly talk to us anymore, you don't hang out with us outside business hours…"

"Maybe I don't like being a fifth wheel," AJ pointed out.

His friend looked startled. "Wait, what? Is that really what you feel like?"

AJ didn't answer for a moment. Truth was, he hadn't given it much thought, but now that he reflected on this past year, he was shocked to realize he *did* feel that way. He adored Darcy and Skyler—he really, truly did—but any and all bro-time had ceased to exist once Reed and Gage had gotten into committed relationships.

"Yeah, I guess I do," he admitted. "I mean, when was the last time you, me, and Gage grabbed drinks at Paddy's?"

Reed voiced a protest. "Just a few weeks ago. Don't you rem—"

"*Without* Darcy and Sky," he cut in. "I mean, don't get me wrong. You know I love them, and I'm not saying I don't want them around, but…" He shrugged again. "You and Gage are in relationship mode now. And I'm not."

Deep shame furrowed Reed's rugged features. "Shit. You're right. We've been living in our own little bubble, huh?"

"Sort of. But whatever. It's cool." AJ rose from his chair and tucked his cell phone in his pocket.

"No, it's not." Reed raked a hand over the stubble on his chin, visibly upset. "We've been acting like assholes."

"Naah, no more than usual."

The good-natured jab didn't appease his friend. "We're

assholes," Reed said firmly. "And screw that. I'm sorry. Starting now, there'll be no more of this fifth-wheel bullshit. I promise to pull my head out of my ass and be a better friend."

AJ softened his tone. "You're a great friend, man. Really. I shouldn't have implied otherwise."

"What's the rush?" Reed demanded as AJ reached for the doorknob. "We're in the middle of something here."

"I've got somewhere I need to be. We'll talk later, okay?"

"No, *not* okay." Reed made a frustrated noise. "You know, the friend thing goes both ways, bro. You never used to be this fucking secretive. And yeah, fine, I'll own up to being a preoccupied ass. Gage, too. But we've been trying to talk to you for weeks, and you keep pushing us away."

The familiar weight of guilt bore down on AJ's shoulders. Damn it. He couldn't deny the accusation, because it was 100 percent true. He *had* been pushing them away.

"You're right." He dropped his hand from the door and exhaled in a rush. "Look, I *am* seeing someone, all right?"

"Ha! I knew it!"

"But it's not serious," he added, "which is why I haven't brought her around."

"It's not serious?" Reed shook his head skeptically. "Dude, you're all about serious."

AJ shook his head right back. "Not this time. Neither one of us wants a relationship."

"But you're, like, Mr. Relationship. *I* was the manwhore in the friendship, remember?" The lines in Reed's forehead deepened. "Were we *Freaky Friday'd* and nobody told me?"

AJ had to grin. "Maybe." He hurried on before Reed could hurl another question his way. "It's no big deal, okay? I'm having a little fun, and that's all there is to it."

"If you say so." Reed hesitated. "I still feel shitty about that fifth-wheel thing. How about you, me, and Gage grab some beers tomorrow? We can make it a dudes' night." He sighed. "God knows Darce and Skyler have enough girls' nights. It can be our turn to gossip about *them*."

"Sounds good." AJ turned the knob and ducked out of the office. "But I really do have to run now. I'll text you tomorrow, 'kay?"

Although talking to Reed had succeeded in alleviating the burden of unhappiness he hadn't even realized he'd been carrying, all thoughts of his friends flew out of AJ's mind as he left the club. The eagerness to see Brett had quickly taken over, bringing a spring of anticipation to his step.

A few minutes later, he was typing the bar address into the Jeep's GPS and planning out the fastest route to get to Brett.

There was a bouncer manning the door at Donnelly's.

That was the first indication that something might be amiss, because AJ hadn't encountered many bouncers in Boston's pub scene. Someone inside to check IDs, sure, but never posted at the door.

And when he noticed the clipboard in the bulky man's hand, the situation looked even less promising.

Wary, AJ approached the door, only for a meaty hand to rise up and stop him. "Sorry," the man barked. "Pub's closed for a private party."

Wonderful. Brett could've warned him that Jordan's birthday shindig was a private affair. He peered at the main window, but it was fully tinted, making it impossible to see inside. Still, she had to be in there somewhere. And she definitely wouldn't have left him in the lurch.

"I should be on the list," he told the bouncer. "Name's AJ Walsh."

The man's gaze lowered to his clipboard, and then he gave

a brisk shake of the head, officially squashing all the faith AJ had placed in Brett.

"You're not on the list, bro. Sorry."

"Look, my—" The word *girlfriend* got stuck in his throat, so he rephrased himself. "My friend's in there. Everyone's expecting me."

"What's your friend's name?" The bouncer's dubious expression said he wasn't buying what AJ was selling.

"Brett."

A pair of bushy black eyebrows soared. "For real?"

"Yes. For real." He couldn't stop the edge in his tone. "Why?"

"You don't seem like Brett's type."

Of course. Yet another person making a judgment call about the "type" of man he was.

"Wait here. I'll be right back." With a little smirk, the bouncer ducked into the bar and left AJ outside like a chump.

Less than a minute later, the enormous man returned and held open the door. "Go on in. Brett's coming to meet you."

Thank fuck. AJ had been worried he'd be forced to hang out with Mountain Man until someone from Jordan's party wandered out and vouched for him. Brett's cell had gone to voice mail when he'd called to let her know he was on his way, which wasn't a surprise—these past couple weeks he'd discovered that the infuriating woman never remembered to charge her phone.

AJ stepped into the small, wood-paneled entryway, where he was instantly greeted by the sound of classic rock blasting out of the pub's speakers. Loud voices and bursts of laughter drifted out of the main room, but he didn't get a chance to go there, because another behemoth of a man obstructed his line of vision.

"Well, damn," the guy drawled. "Dude, I don't know who you are, but I sure as hell ain't complaining."

AJ faltered. The person in front of him was a complete stranger. A very big, very terrifying stranger. He was six five, if not taller, with tattoo-covered arms, silver piercings through his lip and both eyebrows, and a body-builder physique that AJ would've been scared shitless of if the two men had been in an MMA cage.

"I...think there might be some kind of mistake..." Frowning, he took an uneasy step back, but a hand clapped over his arm to stop him.

"Fuck no," the stranger exclaimed. "C'mon, join the party. The more the merrier, Blondie."

AJ had no time to object. He was being dragged into the pub, and the hand on his arm might as well have been a steel vise.

Half a second later, there was no doubt in his mind that he was in the wrong frickin' place.

Forty or so people crowded the dim-lit room—nearly all male. He spotted maybe four or five females in the mix. None of which were Brett. And of course, who could miss the huge green banner draped across the massive stone fireplace on the other side of the cozy room?

The one that read: CONGRATULATIONS, LIAM AND STEVE!

The two men's names were written inside a big red heart.

AJ's gaze darted from the crowd of men, to the streamers and balloons, to the makeshift dance floor, until finally it landed on the ten-tiered cake sitting on the sleek oak bar counter...which proudly featured two tuxedo-clad figurines on the top layer.

Two grooms.

"Yeah, I'm totally in the wrong place—" he started.

The grip on his arm tightened as the man it belonged to broke out in a smile. "C'mon, Blondie, let's dance."

The next thing he knew, the grinning behemoth pulled him onto the dance floor.

Chapter Thirteen

AJ was waiting outside Brett's door when she reached the top of the staircase. With his back against the wall and his long legs stretched out before him, it appeared as if he'd been sitting there for quite some time.

"Hey," she said as he hopped to his feet. "Where the hell were you tonight?"

She tried not to convey just how annoyed she was, but jeez, she did *not* like being stood up. She'd been ready to leave the party an hour after she'd gotten there, but she'd hung around at the pub for *two* extra hours waiting for AJ to arrive. Two hours of listening to Jessica babble on about makeup and shoes. Two hours of watching Jordan get drunker and drunker, a state that never failed to lead to an argument between him and Jessica. Which it had. A very loud one, too.

And she got home to find AJ hunkered down on her doorstep like a street urchin?

"I waited for hours," she said accusingly, her annoyance spilling over before she could stop it.

"I've been calling for hours," he shot back. "Why didn't

you answer your phone?"

"Because it died right after we talked." She scowled as she rummaged in her purse for her keys. "Seriously, dude, what the hell happened to you? Jordan was bummed that you didn't show."

"Oh, I showed," he mumbled.

Brett yanked her key ring out of her bag. "You did not. Trust me, I'd know if you did. Unlike you, *I* was actually there."

"*You* sent me to the wrong place," he said darkly. "I'm still trying to figure out if it was an honest mistake or if you were pulling a prank on me."

Her irritation dissolved.

Cue: confusion.

"I have no idea what you're talking about." She strode inside and flicked the light switch, then kicked off her heels and spun around to face him. "I think *you* might be pranking *me*."

"Ha. Says the prank master." AJ glared at her. "I went to Donnelly's, Brett. You weren't there."

"Of course I wasn't."

"Ha!" he said again. "See?"

"Because Jordan's thing was at *Donaghy's*."

"You said Donnelly's."

"Nuh-uh, I said Donaghy's. Do-na-ghy's." Her victorious smile faded when she noticed the miserable look on his face. "Why? What happened at Donnelly's?"

"What didn't happen at Donnelly's?" was his muttered response.

Without another word, he stalked to the kitchen and rifled through her fridge like he owned it. He pulled out a bottle of Heineken, the last of the six-pack he'd brought over the other night, then twisted off the cap and took a hearty swig.

Brett watched his strong throat as he swallowed. She frowned when a flash of silver winked beneath the overhead light.

"AJ…" She spoke in a cautious tone. "Is that *glitter* in your hair?"

"Yeah." He chugged some more beer. "The stripper was throwing it around during his set."

Brett fell silent.

She had no clue which part of that sentence to deconstruct first.

"I'm sorry, but did you say *stripper*?" She paused. "*His* set?" Another pause. "What exactly did you do tonight?"

He set down the bottle, and his cheeks hollowed as if he were grinding his molars. "I went to an engagement party for Liam and Steve."

Brett pressed her lips together. Fought hard not to laugh. "Ah. Okay. And who are Liam and Steve?"

The teeth grinding continued. "Just a couple of dudes."

"Uh-huh. I figured as much. And how did you meet these 'dudes'?"

"Well, I went to Donnelly's"—he shot her a dirty look—"like you told me to—"

"I said Donaghy's!"

"—but you weren't there, and there was a mix-up at the door when I gave them your name. Turns out there *was* a Brett inside, except it was a man, and he was like seven feet tall and wicked-terrifying." AJ's breath spiraled out in a rush. "The next thing I know, I'm surrounded by a bunch of guys celebrating their friends' engagement, and then Man Brett wouldn't take no for an answer and pulls me onto the dance floor. But he ended up being a really nice guy, and—"

Brett lost it.

A howl of laughter ripped out of her throat as her body doubled over in hysterics. She couldn't even focus on AJ's face anymore, because tears were running down her cheeks.

"Oh my God. You *danced* with him?" Every word popped

out in the form of a wheeze.

AJ's tone took on a defensive edge. "He was a good dancer!"

"And then a stripper showed up?" she wailed between giggles.

"Quit laughing at me, woman. And no, the stripper was later."

"Later?" She clutched her side, howling again. "How long were you *there*?"

"A few hours." AJ shrugged. "After the dancing, Man Brett and Frankie talked me into a darts tournament, so we did that for a while—I won, by the way—and then it was time for the speeches. Son of a bitch, you would have bawled your eyes out during Liam's speech. So fucking poignant."

Brett's legs buckled under her. She collapsed on the tiled floor in a heap of giggles, barely able to hear him over the sounds bursting out of her throat.

"The stripper showed up after that, and I guess he was pretty good? I've never seen a male stripper in action, so I don't have anything to compare him to. The guy was all about the glitter, though." AJ dragged his hand through his hair, and a few sprinkles of silver danced off and sparkled in the light.

Brett's laughs turned to hiccups as she swiped at her watery cheeks. "Oh God. I'm going to pee my pants. I can't believe you accidentally went to a gay engagement party—and *liked* it."

AJ loomed over her, frowning at the sad mess she'd become. "They were good guys. Well, except for Tony—he was a total dick. Turns out he used to date Steve before Steve and Liam hooked up, and he's clearly still carrying a torch for him. He was scowling in the corner like an asshole the entire time."

Another high-pitched wail flew out.

"So yeah, I got a bunch of their numbers. We're all going

to hang out again, I think. And I'm—" He stopped abruptly.

"Please. Oh God, please finish that sentence."

There was a resigned flicker in his eyes as she hiccupped loudly. "I'm now an official member of the Roxbury Lions."

Her lips trembled. "The Roxbury Lions?"

"Yeah. It's, uh, an all-gay amateur rugby league. Season starts in July."

Brett didn't think she could laugh any harder, but oh Lord, she did. Her stomach hurt as she curled up on the kitchen floor, unable to stop picturing the images AJ had described. When she felt herself being hauled to her feet, she giggled even louder, burying her face against AJ's chest as she shuddered uncontrollably.

Eventually she became aware that he was laughing too, the husky sounds warming the top of her head as he rested both hands on her lower back.

"Fine, I guess it is kinda funny." He chuckled. "It definitely wasn't what I expected to be doing tonight."

"Oh my God. You're one of a kind, AJ," she mumbled into his chest. "One of a fucking kind."

"I am?"

She rubbed her tear-soaked cheeks and tilted her head up to look at him. "I'm not sure other men would have handled that as well as you."

He drew his brows together in a frown. "What, did you think I was a homophobe?"

"Of course not. But even the most tolerant hetero guys might get freaked out by something like that. People don't like to step out of their comfort zones." She leaned up and brushed her lips over his jaw. "I like that you were able to do that and have a good time."

"Hmmm…well…" His voice became thoughtful. "I *do* feel a tad intimidated. Like maybe my masculinity has been threatened."

She caught the wicked curve of his mouth. "Liar."

"I'm serious." He swept a possessive hand over her tailbone before dragging it down to pinch her ass. "I think you might need to help me out. You know, remind me how much I love women…"

"Oh really? How?"

In the blink of an eye, the air in the kitchen transformed from light with humor to thick with sex.

"I'm sure you can figure something out after you undo my pants."

…

AJ had never seen a more beautiful view than Brett sinking to her knees in front of him. With her cheeks still flushed from her fit of laughter and her dark eyes burning with passion, she was temptation personified. A perfect, heart-stoppingly sexy picture he would happily take to his death.

"You poor thing," she murmured, both hands poised on his belt buckle. "Not feeling so masculine, huh?"

He hissed when she slipped the belt free, deliberately rubbing the heel of her hand over his erection. She damn well knew *exactly* how masculine he was feeling at the moment. His rock-hard cock was all the evidence she needed.

And no, he hadn't been intimidated in the slightest back at Donnelly's, at least not after he'd accepted the situation and gave up on trying to reach Brett. He'd actually had a pretty fun time.

"How on earth am I going to make it better?" Brett peered up with a mocking smile, while her fingers eased down his zipper.

He voiced a helpful suggestion. "Your mouth on my dick would be a good start."

She laughed, and the sweet sound was like music to his

ears. Christ, he loved hearing her laugh. Seeing her bent over backward a minute ago had been like stepping into a ray of sunshine. It had warmed his entire body, made him want to join her on the floor and roll around like a kid with her.

"And what do I get in return?" she teased.

"My dick in your mouth." He wiggled his eyebrows as if to say *duh*, and got the desired response. Another melodic laugh, this one snaking into his chest and circling his heart.

She heaved an exaggerated sigh. "I *guess* I can live with that."

A second later, she had his erection in hand, and neither of them was capable of doing much talking after that.

AJ groaned when she wrapped her lips around him. Goddamn it. There was no greater feeling in the world.

Brett's mouth was absolute heaven. Her tongue was pure sin. And she knew exactly how to use both, wasting no time in kindling the arousal that burned in his blood. Long, teasing glides along his shaft, until it was slick with moisture and throbbing with impatience. She sucked on the tip, and AJ almost keeled over from pleasure.

His fingers tangled in her hair, hips flexing as he tried to drive deeper.

But his eager attempt only caused her to release him. "Oh, baby, you need it bad, don't you?"

"Fuck. Yes." He shuddered when she rubbed her thumb over the base of his shaft. "No teasing tonight, angel. Give it to me."

"I think it's the other way around," she said in a throaty voice. "Give it to *me*. *Now*."

Her lips were back with a tight suction and deep strokes guaranteed to blow his mind. AJ cupped the back of her head and thrust into her wet, willing mouth. She dug her short fingernails into his ass cheeks as she swallowed him up, her muffled sounds of pleasure vibrating through his cock.

The climax roared through him like a freight train, turning his knees to jelly. His seed shot out and she tightened her lips around him, sucking so hard he was surprised his brains didn't leak out. His entire world dissolved in a rush of bliss that flowed through his veins and fogged up his mind, until all he could focus on was Brett. Her lips, her tongue, her soft breaths and tiny whimpers.

He stroked her hair, needing to touch her, using the tender caress to show her just how hard she'd rocked his world right now. God knew his vocal chords weren't capable of expressing it.

When his heart rate steadied and his vision cleared, he pulled out gently and hauled her to her feet. He kissed her, tasted himself on her lips, and another shudder racked his body.

"I…" His voice was so hoarse he had to clear his throat. "I think we should keep doing this."

"You mean, I should keep blowing you?" With a saucy smile, she brought her hand to his groin and circled his still-hard cock. "Sure, I'd love to. How many more times would you like me to do it tonight? Five? Ten?"

He wheezed out a laugh. "Fifteen. But that's not what I meant."

She glanced up at him, quizzical.

"I think we should keep seeing each other. Even after the three weeks are up."

Brett let go of his erection, and he could see he'd caught her off guard. Hell, he'd caught *himself* off guard. The idea of amending their temporary status had been floating around in his head ever since he'd told her about Joey, but he hadn't planned on acting on it.

"You want us to date?" she said slowly.

AJ nodded.

"Why?"

He was as bewildered as she was, and he struggled to vocalize his emotions. "I like spending time with you. I like more than just the sex part. We have fun together, don't we?"

"Yeah, we do." She paused. "But…I don't know. I'm going to be super busy if my dad lets me run the new shop."

"I know. And I'm not suggesting we make things any more serious. I just want to keep doing what we're doing. If you're too busy to see me, just say so and we'll hang out on a night when you're free. I won't push you to give me more than you're willing to give."

Her forehead crinkled. "Why?"

"Why what?"

"Why do you want to keep seeing me? I thought I wasn't your type."

Her quiet remark nearly did him in. His chest clenched, aching as he realized he'd hurt her when he'd implied that she wasn't someone he would consider dating. But he hadn't known her back then, not the way he knew her now.

"I won't lie. You're not like the women I've dated in the past," he admitted. "They didn't dress like you, or challenge me like you"—he had to grin—"or fuck like you."

She smirked. "I am phenomenal in bed, I know."

"Damn right you are." He paused. "I'm not thinking about the future. Let's just take it slow and see where things go."

Brett went quiet, doing what she always did whenever she was deep in thought. Bit her lip, wrinkled her forehead, fidgeted with her hands. It was so fucking adorable, and at that moment, he knew with certainty that he'd made the right decision by broaching the subject.

He wasn't ready to say good-bye to Brett Conlon yet.

"Okay," she said. "We're dating."

The evil smile she followed up with sparked his suspicion. He'd learned never to trust her when she got that look on her face.

"And as my new boyfriend, your first order of business is to give me an orgasm," Brett announced. "A really good one, too."

"An orgasm, huh? And a *good* one, to boot? That's asking a lot." He slipped his hand beneath her dress and stroked one firm thigh.

"It's a daunting task," she agreed. "I mean, you'll have to work very hard. We both know your skills aren't up to par yet."

"Up to par? Fuck that." In one swift motion, AJ dropped to his knees and wrenched her panties down her legs. "I don't shoot par, Brett. With me, you get a hole in one. Every. Damn. Time."

Then he buried his face between her thighs and proved it to her.

Chapter Fourteen

"One year." Two words. That was all Brett's father uttered as he settled in her chair and crossed his big arms over his big chest.

It took an outrageous amount of willpower not to squeal in happiness. Or give a fist pump and spin around like a little kid. But Brett did her damndest to control her excitement, especially since her father was staring at her with that super-serious, super-stern expression.

"You have one year to show me what you can do," Jimmy Conlon continued. "I'll be working with you during the first month to teach you everything. Payroll, management, stock, all that boring stuff." He cocked his head in challenge, but Brett wasn't the slightest bit fazed.

She'd done it. It had taken six long months, but she'd finally proved to him that she could be trusted.

"I'm going to love every boring second of it," she vowed.

His lips twitched. "I think you actually mean that."

"I do." She flung herself at the chair, wrapping her arms around his broad shoulders to hug him tightly. "Thank you.

I promise I won't let you down, Dad. By the end of the year, Conlon Ink North will bring in more money than the other two locations combined. Just you watch."

"Don't get ahead of yourself, princess. Running a small business is a lot harder than you think. With that said, I do believe you'll work your butt off to make it happen." He got up from the chair and pulled her up with him, his voice going brusque. "I know I've been hard on you, but that's because you're my little girl. I guess that makes your old man a hypocrite, though. I let the boys run wild, because that's what I did when I was their age, but I expected more of you."

"I know." She swallowed. "I'm sorry for all the trouble I caused you."

Her shame was reflected back at her in her dad's eyes. "I might have judged you too harshly," he admitted. "I mean, when Mikey was your age, I bailed him out of jail on a weekly basis."

"Really?" she said in surprise.

"Oh yeah. I'm surprised the kid didn't turn out to be a criminal. But I wanted better for you, princess. We both know you get your stubbornness from your mom, but your wild side…that came from me, and I tried to hammer it outta you. I didn't want you to end up like me, I guess."

"I'd be *proud* to end up like you," she said fiercely. "You're smart and successful and you raised great kids and had an amazing marriage. What more could I want?"

"I was a punk before I met your mother," he said gruffly.

"But you grew up." She paused. "I've grown up, too. I promise, I'm going to make you proud."

"I already am proud." He ruffled her hair, and his indulgent smile warmed Brett's heart. "I love you, princess."

"Love you, too, Daddy." The excitement returned, making her bounce on the balls of her feet. "So what now? When do we start?"

"Tomorrow, nine a.m. I want you at the new site with me. The grand opening is in a month, so we've got a lot of work ahead of us. Tomorrow we're talking to the contractors, and I want to meet with a few artists, too." A frown suddenly marred his lips. "You should know—Mathis stopped by with a résumé yesterday."

Brett froze.

Troy? He'd applied for a job at the new shop?

"Are you serious?" she exclaimed.

"Don't worry, I made it clear there's no chance in hell I'd let him work for us. But I'm not thrilled that he's back in the picture, princess."

"He's not. I swear. He stopped by a couple weeks ago when Rob and I were closing up, and I told him exactly where I stand. I have zero interest in seeing him ever again. I'm with AJ now."

And she wasn't even lying. Figure that one out.

Brett still couldn't wrap her head around the notion that she and AJ were officially dating now—and that she wasn't freaked out about it.

She hadn't wanted a relationship. A clear head and a new lifestyle were all she'd been interested in, at least before AJ Walsh had snuck through her defenses and made her reconsider.

When she was with him, she felt...centered. Not like in her past relationships, when she'd been wholly consumed, too caught up in them to notice the chaos she was causing and the mistakes she was making

It was different with AJ. When she'd cooked him dinner the other night, he'd actually *thanked* her. And when she'd canceled their plans yesterday because she had to work on a design for a client, he hadn't tried coercing her into blowing off work for him. He'd just accepted that she was busy and wished her luck on finishing the sketch, which was something

Troy never would have done in a million years.

She didn't know why she'd found a balance with AJ that she hadn't found with anyone else, but she sure as hell wasn't complaining.

"Anyway," her dad said, "I need to take off now. Gotta pop over to Mikey's shop and help him out. One of his artists called in sick." He tweaked a strand of her hair. "I'll see you tomorrow. Nine o'clock sharp."

"I'll be there."

The second her father was gone, Brett let out a whoop and broke out in a happy dance. If anyone had peeked behind her curtain, they would have laughed their asses off, but she didn't care how silly she looked. She was going to run her own tattoo parlor. She'd *done* it, damn it.

She hurried to the counter and grabbed her phone, needing to share her excitement with someone. "The shop's mine!" she blurted out the moment AJ answered the phone.

"Well, damn!" His deep voice slid into her ear and brought a rush of warmth to her heart. "That's great news, baby. See, I told you there was nothing to worry about."

Brett rested her hip against the counter. "I'm so relieved," she confessed. "But I'm kind of nervous, too. My dad and I are hiring artists tomorrow. I have no clue how to interview people!"

"It's easy," he assured her. "I do it all the time when I'm hiring bar staff. I can give you some tips if you want. Questions you should ask, that sorta thing."

A wave of gratitude swelled in her stomach. "You'd really do that?"

"Absolutely. But first, I have to take you out to celebrate." Hesitation rippled over the line. "I know we were planning to go for dinner later, but can you meet up earlier? I'm having drinks with my partners and their girlfriends at the club tonight, just a private friend hangout. If you want to come by, we can celebrate with the guys for a bit, and then have dinner and celebrate some more."

He wanted her to hang out with his friends? Whoa. He really *was* serious about this dating thing.

The invitation was slightly unnerving, though. AJ's friends were used to seeing him with "wholesome" girls, and Brett wasn't sure what they'd think of her. What if they hated her?

At the same time, she was curious to meet them. Not just because AJ talked about Reed and Gage all the time, but also because she was dying for more glimpses into his life. For weeks he'd been compartmentalizing—their fling in one corner, the rest of his life in the other. And she'd been cool with that. No point in getting attached when things were just temporary.

Now that they were dating for real, all bets were off.

"Sure, that sounds like fun," she answered. "I'm actually done at six today. I only have two clients, and Rob's new apprentice is handling the walk-ins so I don't have to stick around. What time should I come?"

"Seven thirtyish okay? We can do drinks for an hour or so, then catch a late dinner?"

"Awesome. I'll see you later then."

"Brett?" he said before she could hang up. "I'm proud of you."

Brett was touched beyond words as she set down her phone. *Two* people had told her they were proud of her today. It'd been a long time since she'd heard those words once, let alone twice.

The rest of her day flew by. Whether from giddiness or excitement, she didn't know, but it felt like seven thirty rolled around in minutes rather than hours.

She'd stopped by her place to shower and change, and as she approached the club through the staff door in the back, a strange prickle of nervousness poked at her. She'd worn a strapless black dress, her trademark leather boots, and a shock of red lipstick, but suddenly she felt overdressed. Or maybe underdressed. Hell, she had no idea what AJ's friends would be wearing. She didn't know what to expect from them, either. She remembered Reed from high school, but they'd never exchanged a single word back then, and who knew what this Gage guy was like. And AJ's ex-girlfriend. Crap. She'd be there, too.

Brett swallowed to bring moisture to her dry mouth and ran a shaky hand through her hair. Okay. Enough. She was not the kind of woman who worried about what other people thought of her.

AJ had wanted her to come, and that was all she ought to care about.

She texted AJ to let him know she was outside, and a minute later, the heavy metal door swung open and Brett was being tugged into a pair of warm, muscular arms.

He hugged her tight, then kissed her until she was utterly breathless. "Hi," he said huskily.

She smiled. "Hi."

"So how does it feel to be the new manager of Conlon Ink, North End location?"

"Incredible. How does it feel to be the boy toy of the new manager of Conlon Ink, North End location?"

"Frickin' awesome." His green eyes twinkled. "By the way, you look gorgeous."

Brett's nerves dissolved like sugar in water. Yep. Screw what his friends thought. The blatant admiration on AJ's face was reward enough for showing up tonight.

"Come on, everyone's already here," he said, taking her hand. "Reed just cracked open a bottle of Dom."

"Oooh, you're bringing out the good stuff tonight."

He grinned. "Only the best for my angel."

"Bull crap. I was a last-minute addition. You were gonna

get fancy regardless."

It was jarring to walk through the club without feeling the *thump* of a bass line beneath her feet or encountering a cacophony of voices in the main space. Brett had questioned AJ and his partners' business plan when he'd explained that Sin was closed Monday through Wednesday. It seemed like a waste of profit potential to her, but apparently the tactic had only boosted Sin's reputation for being hip and exclusive.

Voices wafted out of the second-floor VIP lounge as she and AJ ascended the staircase. Another jab of nervousness stabbed her belly. This was it. Her first "appearance" as AJ's girlfriend.

The two couples sitting in the padded red booth looked harmless enough. One of the men—Reed, she realized—had his arm slung around the shoulders of a pretty woman with strawberry-blond hair. The other, a guy with intense gray eyes, had a blue-eyed brunette in his lap and was whispering something in her ear when AJ and Brett approached.

"This is Brett," AJ announced, resting a possessive hand on her hip.

Introductions quickly went around, and then Brett found herself seated next to AJ, as the brunette—Skyler—climbed off Gage's lap to pour her a glass of champagne.

"Why do you look so familiar?" Reed studied her face, as if trying to place her.

"Brett went to school with us," AJ told his friend. "She's Rob Conlon's sister. You remember Rob, right?"

"No shit, you're Rob's sister? How's that guy doing?"

Brett was momentarily distracted by the other man's ruggedly handsome face. Reed's grin only emphasized the masculine planes and crinkles of humor around his vivid blue eyes. She remembered him being a lot scruffier back in the day, and definitely not as buff. But all the men in the booth were built in the same lean, muscular way. She would have loved to see them in a fight. AJ, especially. She got the feeling he'd look extraordinary behind the chain-link walls of an MMA cage.

"He's doing good," she told Reed. "He runs our family's tattoo parlor in Southie."

When she said the word *tattoo*, she noticed Darcy staring at her arms, and the tiny frown on the blonde's face raised Brett's hackles.

"Did your brother do those for you?" Darcy asked. Her tone was pleasant, but Brett detected a cool note beneath the surface.

"He did the stars. My dad did the angel, though."

"That's serious talent right there," Gage spoke up, impressed. "What's the name of the shop?"

"Conlon Ink." She took a hesitant sip of champagne. Sometimes she had a beer or two with AJ when he came by, but for the most part, she hadn't been drinking much lately, and the last thing she wanted was to get tipsy in front of AJ's friends.

Gage nodded. "I've heard of it. You guys have a good rep." He gestured to the elaborate black flames inked on both his arms. "Got my ink done at Razor's. You know them?"

Her spine stiffened, but she hoped nobody had noticed. Troy worked at Razor's, or at least he had six months ago. The fact that he was handing out résumés put his current job status in question. Not that she cared.

"They do good work," she said vaguely.

Darcy spoke up again. "So you and AJ went to high school together… How did you two reconnect?"

"We ran into each other here, actually."

"And now you're dating." This time, the other woman's iciness was impossible to miss.

"Now we're dating," Brett confirmed.

She couldn't help herself—she met Darcy's eyes in

challenge, silently daring her to object or contradict or who the hell knew what. It was obvious AJ's ex wasn't thrilled about Brett's presence, but the blonde didn't take the bait. She simply picked up her glass and took a dainty sip.

Despite the small victory, Brett got the unsettling feeling that it was going to be a *very* long hour.

...

"You okay?" AJ studied Brett's face as they entered her apartment.

He'd had to cancel their dinner reservations because Brett had changed her mind about going out. She'd suggested they order in instead, winking as if to imply that it was for sex purposes, but he'd seen right through her.

"I'm fine," she said, the epitome of noncommittal.

She was lying. He knew she wasn't fine. And he knew why.

"Bull," he said softly. "You're upset, and I don't blame you. Darcy was acting…" He trailed off, unsure how to phrase it.

"I think the word you're looking for is *bitchy*."

She bent over to unzip one boot, which caused her dress to ride up her thighs. Her koi fish tattoo peeked out enticingly, but he forced himself to stay focused. He watched as she kicked each boot onto the mat in the front hall, her previously casual body language stiffening to reveal the hurt she'd been trying to hide.

"I don't know what got into her," AJ admitted. "She's not usually so…"

"Bitchy?" Brett supplied.

Fine. He'd call a spade a spade. Darcy had been bitchier than he'd ever seen her, and for a woman who was usually sweeter than cherry pie, AJ had been shocked by the sudden personality shift. Darcy's hostility toward Brett had been palpable, so much so that Reed had even apologized to AJ in private before he and Brett had left Sin.

Was Darcy jealous?

The thought had occurred to him somewhere between the first and last barbed remark she'd tossed in Brett's direction, but it made no fucking sense to him. He and Darcy had only dated for five months, and any idiot could see that she was madly in love with Reed. Since she'd started dating his best friend, she'd given AJ no indication that she still had feelings for him. Which made her antagonism of Brett completely baffling.

"God, you can't be *that* clueless."

Brett's grumble interrupted his train of thought, making him frown. "What do you mean?"

"Your ex-girlfriend doesn't think I'm good enough for you."

His brow creased even harder. "That's not true."

"Yes, it is. That's why she was glaring at me the whole time like I was robbing her house or something. And all those comments about what a good guy you are, directly followed by snippy jabs about my tats or my job or the fact that I'm *three whole years* younger than you? She might as well have paid for a billboard and pasted it all over the city. In neon pink."

Although her blunt evaluation of the evening disturbed him, AJ couldn't deny it was pretty much how things had gone down.

"I get it. She's your ex, and she's protective of you." Brett shrugged. "But with that said, don't blame me when I say I'm not interested in hanging out with her again."

Guilt dripped down his spine, along with a hefty dose of indignation on Brett's behalf. She hadn't deserved to be treated like an unwanted intruder, and he definitely planned on having a talk with Darcy the next time he saw her.

"C'mere." He opened his arms, beckoning at her. "Forget about Darcy. It doesn't matter what she thinks or why she decided to act like a dick. All that matters is what I think."

Brett stepped into his waiting embrace and wrapped her slender arms around his waist. A pleading note—shocking and unexpected—wobbled in her voice. "And what *do* you think?"

"I think you're beautiful." He stroked her hair, then grazed his fingers over the angel on her upper arm. "I think you're smart. And strong. And confident."

He moved his hands lower, cupping her ass. "I think you're sexy." He angled her body into his groin so she could feel his hard-on. "I think you turn me on like no other woman ever has."

"Including Darcy?" The question was muffled against his chest.

"Including Darcy." He kissed her neck, inhaling the scent of body lotion and a fragrance that was uniquely Brett. Spicy and hot and addictive. "Everything about you gets me hard. The sound of your voice, the way you smell. You're perfect."

"I'm not perfect."

"Oh, but you are." AJ slipped his hand beneath her dress and delicately pushed aside the crotch of her panties. When he felt the moisture pooled at her opening, he groaned. "Perfect," he repeated.

Brett rocked into his touch, a breathless sound leaving her lips. He loved the noises she made when he put his hands on her. Loved knowing that he had the power to make her tremble, moan, beg.

He swept his fingers upward and sought out her clit, finding it hot and swollen to the touch. As he tickled the taut bud, Brett's eyelids fluttered, and she let out a dreamy sigh.

"So good," she whispered. "Keep doing that."

"Only gonna get better, baby."

AJ slid down to his knees and circled her shapely ankles with his hands, rubbing his thumbs over her smooth skin. She shivered, then yelped when he tugged one leg and lifted it up to his shoulder, fully exposing her to him.

"Oh yeah," he rasped. "So much better."

His pulse raced as he placed a tender kiss on her pretty pink folds, tasting her, exploring. He went down on her right there in the hallway, using his tongue and fingers to make her come apart, which took no time at all. And even as her body continued to tremble from the orgasm, he scooped her into his arms and carried her to the bedroom. Screw dinner. He had more pressing matters on his mind right now.

He stripped off her dress, followed by every stitch of clothing covering him. Then he laid her down on the bed, and for the next hour, proceeded to kiss every inch of her body. Her tattoos. Her nipples. Her pussy again. The hurt look on Brett's face had been branded into his memory, and he was desperate to erase it, desperate to show her that she *was* important. That she deserved to be adored and appreciated and worshipped, damn it.

"Oh God, what are you *doing* to me?" she choked out when his tongue yet again circled her clit.

"Everything," he said simply.

Slipping two fingers into her tight channel, he resumed his single-minded objective to make her come again. Christ, she really was perfect. Soft and warm and beautiful, melting into the mattress as he gently coaxed her back to the edge.

His cock was rock hard and raring to go, and when he finally climbed up her body and slid inside her, he almost lost it on the first thrust.

"I love this," Brett whispered. Her arms looped around his neck and her legs circled his waist, the heels of her feet digging into his buttocks.

She arched her hips, and a shock of pleasure raced down

his spine and tingled in his balls. Slow. He had to go slow. Make it last. Make it *good*.

But Brett had clearly had enough of the painstaking pace he'd set. Her ass rose off the bed to meet his thrusts, her legs trapping him against her, giving him no choice but to thrust back. To wildly grind into her and make both of them moan with abandon.

Ecstasy twisted in his gut, spilling over before he could stop it. AJ came with a groan, burying his face in her neck as release barreled through him in pulsing waves and stole every coherent thought from his head.

Later, after they'd devoured fifty dollars worth of Chinese takeout, they nestled together in each other's arms, Brett's cheek pressed to his bare chest as he lazily twined a strand of her hair between his fingers.

Her warm breath fanned over his pecs. "Why don't you ever want to hang out at your place?"

AJ was surprised it had taken her this long to voice the question, but he supposed there was no avoiding it now that they were dating.

Dating. Man, the concept still felt so foreign to him. He hadn't expected to get attached to this woman. Hadn't expected the gut-wrenching stab he'd felt last week when he'd imagined saying good-bye to her.

"I like it better here," he answered, absently stroking her back.

"Why?"

"I don't know... Your place feels...lived in, I guess. Welcoming. It has personality—*your* personality."

"And yours doesn't?"

"Not really." He paused. "My mother decorated it, and

honestly, it's never felt like home to me."

Brett sounded upset. "Didn't you have any say? You didn't pick out furniture or colors or artwork?"

"Nope. She did it all."

"You could have said no," she pointed out.

"I could've, but I didn't. I guess I didn't see the harm in letting her have her way. I'd already let her down about so many other things. If decorating my apartment made her happy, then I figured, why not."

"But it's *your* home." Brett raised herself up on her elbow. "You should have done it your way."

"Maybe, but I didn't, and now I've gotta live with it. Or *in* it. Whatever."

He shrugged, ready to change the subject, but he didn't get the chance, because loud knocking suddenly blasted through the apartment, causing him and Brett to exchange startled looks.

"What the hell?" she muttered, with a quick glance at the bedside clock.

He followed her gaze, noting that it was nearly midnight. What the hell, indeed.

Brett sat up uneasily and pulled the sheet over her naked breasts. The pounding on the front door didn't let up. It only got louder and more persistent as the door remained unanswered.

And then a muffled male voice reached their ears.

"Brett! Let me in!"

AJ's chest stiffened at the same time Brett's eyes went as wide as Frisbees. "Shit," she blurted out. "*Shit.*"

AJ was out of bed in a heartbeat. "Who is it?" he demanded, his protective urges roaring to life as the voice continued to scream Brett's name.

She met his gaze, anger and horror flashing on her face. "My ex-boyfriend."

Chapter Fifteen

Brett flew off the bed in a frenzied search for something to wear. AJ's T-shirt was the first item her panicked fingers collided with, and she slipped it on in a hurry, only realizing afterward that commandeering his shirt left him with nothing to wear. But she was too panicked to care. Troy's voice continued to reverberate in the apartment, growing more and more desperate by the second.

"Brett! I know you're in there! I saw your car outside! Open the damn door!"

As the pounding on the door escalated, honest-to-God fear pricked at Brett's flesh. Troy hadn't gotten violent with her when they'd been together, but she'd never heard him sound like this before.

"Stay here." AJ's low command penetrated the shrieking alarms going off in her head.

She turned to see him buttoning his black trousers, his blond hair tousled and mouth carved in a deadly line.

Her faculties swiftly returned to her. "No," she blurted out. "You stay here. I'll deal with him."

"If you honestly think I'm going to let you handle this alone, then you're…" He didn't even finish the sentence.

He was already marching out the door.

Brett hurried after him, her panic intensifying when she glimpsed the inflexible set of his broad shoulders. Bare-chested and barefoot, he painted an imposing picture that would go over like a sack of bricks with Troy. Her ex might not have been violent, but he was possessive as hell, and Brett was suddenly terrified of what he'd do when he found another man in her apartment.

AJ, however, didn't seem at all concerned. Once he reached the front hall, he threw open the door and took an intimidating step toward her ex.

So much for rehab—Troy was drunk. Very, very drunk. Brett had borne witness to those bloodshot eyes and stumbling posture countless times before.

But the fury was new.

Red-hot and palpable, blazing hotter when Troy looked from AJ's bare chest to Brett's oversized and very masculine T-shirt.

"What the hell!" he roared. "You're screwing around with some loser while I'm standing outside your door trying to talk to you!"

"What are you doing here?" she shot back. "I already told you—I have no interest in seeing you."

"I don't give a *shit* what you want! Tell this loser to go. We need to talk."

Brett's heart stopped when Troy tried to elbow his way inside, but she'd underestimated AJ's reflexes. In the blink of an eye, he'd shoved the slurring man into the hallway, every muscle in his body flexing with power as he pushed Troy against the wall and jammed his forearm into the man's throat.

"You heard the lady," AJ hissed. "She doesn't want you here." He dug his arm harder, making Troy gasp. "Which means you have five seconds to get your ass out of here before we call the cops."

"Screw you!" was the hoarse response.

Brett lunged at AJ, grabbing onto his waist in an attempt to pull him back. "AJ. Stop," she pleaded. "Let him go."

At the feel of her hands on his skin, his torso relaxed. Slightly. He looked over, and the menacing gleam in his green eyes sent a ripple of shock through her. She'd never seen that look on his face. Lethal and enraged, with a hard glint of protectiveness that evoked an untimely burst of pleasure. He would protect her to his last breath, she realized. Do any damn thing he needed in order to keep her safe.

But there was no way she was letting him.

"He's not worth it," she murmured against his shoulder blades. "Let him go."

AJ's body was straining again, his breathing labored as he twisted his head to meet her gaze. But it was a costly mistake, taking his attention off Troy. Brett's drunken ex was as tall and broad as AJ, and he took advantage of the other man's distraction, wiggling out of AJ's iron grip and unleashing his fist.

Brett cried out as AJ's head was thrown back from the blow. The next thing she knew, she was being manhandled, pushed to the side as AJ sprang to action. Troy was ready for the attack this time, fists swinging wildly as Brett watched in horror.

A crack sliced the air when AJ landed an uppercut on Troy's jaw. Brett had never seen anyone move so fast, and it was hard not to picture that same lethal speed in a fighting cage, those same precise jabs and right hooks as AJ took down an opponent.

The fight was over before it even began. After that first punch, Troy didn't stand a chance in the face of AJ's deadly domination.

With an agonized whimper, Troy raised one hand in surrender, using the other one to frantically swipe at the blood pouring from the lip AJ had just split.

"Get your phone, Brett," AJ said ominously. "It's time to call the police."

"No!" Troy burst out. He stumbled backward, until his shoulders connected with the wall. "Don't call the cops. I'm going. I swear." His rattled eyes darted in Brett's direction, sheer misery making his voice crack. "I just wanted to talk to you, damn it. You can't take this job away from me, baby. Please."

Confusion joined the adrenaline coursing in her blood. "I have no idea what you're talking about."

Her ex ignored her, stammering wildly. "You can't do this to me. I get it—I hurt you. But you can't go around telling every studio in town not to hire me. I'm a good artist, goddamn it! I'm *good*! You can't—"

"I haven't done a damn thing," she interrupted coldly. "I know you tried to apply at our new place, but you're cuckoo-frickin'-crazy if you think my dad would ever hire you. As for the other studios in Boston, did you ever stop to think that maybe the reason nobody's hiring you is because they know what a pathetic screwup you are?"

Troy's entire face collapsed. "I got fired from Razor's, Brett. I *need* this job."

"There is no job. Not at my shop, and clearly nowhere else, either." She inhaled slowly. "You need to go now."

"Or what?" He cast a petulant look at AJ. "You'll sic this crazy mofo on me again?"

"No." She set her jaw. "I'll beat the crap out of you myself."

AJ's faint snicker made Troy's nostrils flare.

"You know what?" he muttered. "Screw you, Brett. Screw *both* of you. I'm not putting up with your BS anymore." His whole body swayed as he stumbled toward the staircase.

"Have a nice life."

Unsteady footsteps echoed down the stairs, followed by the deafening slam of the door below them. As her ex-boyfriend once again walked out of her life, Brett looked over at AJ, unsure of what to say.

She wanted to apologize to him for Troy. She wanted to yell at him for putting himself in harm's way. She wanted to kiss him for sticking up for her.

But then she glimpsed the swollen red mark beneath his cheekbone, and all she wanted to do was take care of him.

"Come on, we should put some ice on that."

Neither of them spoke as they walked inside. In the kitchen, Brett grabbed a bag of frozen peas from the freezer, then pressed it to AJ's cheek.

God, she hated that he'd gotten hurt defending her, but she knew she'd never forget the lightning speed with which he'd moved, or the waves of danger that had rippled in his roped muscles.

And yet she wasn't surprised when he voiced a quick, shame-laced apology.

"I'm sorry. I shouldn't have wailed on him like that."

Frustration clamped around Brett's throat as he once again apologized for who he was. As he once again ducked behind the mask and hid another part of himself from the world.

He'd done it earlier too, when they'd been around his friends. Darcy's coldness had been annoying, but that wasn't the sole reason Brett had been upset when they'd gotten home. She hadn't liked the way AJ had acted at the club. Mr. Good Guy, pouring drinks for everyone, bending over backward to make up for Darcy's hostility, biting back the raunchy remarks he usually had no problem saying to her.

She understood why he felt the need to project that image, but damn it, she didn't like it. She liked AJ exactly the way he was, every complicated facet to him. Sweet and tender. Bold and reckless. Strong and deadly. Indecent and dirty.

"Don't apologize," she said quietly. "He had it coming."

"Oh, a hundred percent. But..." A beat of hesitation. "But I wish you hadn't seen me like that. So out of control."

"You looked very in control to me."

"Yes, but..." He visibly gulped. "I don't want you to be scared of me."

"Scared of you? God, AJ. I could never be scared of you." She dropped the bag of peas on the counter and reached up to cup his strong jaw. "I don't think you realize how good you've been for me."

A tentative smile lifted the corner of his mouth. "Really?"

"This is the healthiest relationship I've ever been in. I'm..." She chewed her lip as she tried to put her emotions into words. "I'm not a pushover when I'm with you, and you don't demand that I devote every second of my time to you. I mean, I see you almost every day, but I'm still focused on work and able to do my job. It's like I've finally found a way to balance life and a relationship." She offered a little grin. "And watching you kick Troy's ass tonight was a major turn-on. Now I'm dying to track down footage of your old fights so I can see some more ass-kicking."

"Yeah?" he murmured.

"Oh yeah." She brushed a kiss on his lips. "You defended me tonight, and I'm very grateful for that. *Troy* was the one who was out of control. I thought I could handle it myself, but now I'm not so sure. I'm glad you were here."

The confession seemed to drain the remaining tension from his body. He sagged into her touch, rubbing his cheeks against her palms. "I'm glad I was here, too."

Brett rested her head on his bare chest. The thump of his heartbeat vibrated against her ear, soothing her.

Let me show you who I am.

The husky words he'd said to her at Sin floated into her mind. He'd kept that promise. He'd shown her exactly who he was that first night, and she found comfort in the knowledge that AJ didn't hide himself from her. But he hid from everyone else. His friends, his family…

Brett didn't like it. She wanted AJ to be as proud of himself as she was of him.

Now she just had to convince him.

Chapter Sixteen

Two Weeks Later

It was Meet the Parents day.

And no, not a movie date featuring one of Brett's all-time favorite films. But by God, she wished it was.

She wasn't ready for this.

Which was more than a little ironic because *she* was the one who'd insisted. Actually, she'd done a lot of insisting these past couple weeks, and she was kind of surprised AJ had put up with it.

When she'd finally been granted access to his sacred apartment last week, she'd promptly taken it upon herself to bring some life to his sterile surroundings, in the form of colorful rugs, throw pillows, and some of her framed drawings.

When she'd discovered what a horrendous cook he was, she'd taught him how to prepare a hearty Irish stew that he could freeze and then nuke as needed.

When she'd found out he didn't own a DVD player, she'd gone out and bought one for him, then proceeded to make him marathon six hours of vampire television.

And when he'd mentioned last night that he was going to his parents' house the following afternoon for lunch, she'd offered to go with him.

AJ hadn't complained about any of it, including her suggestion to meet his parents. He'd hesitated for only a split second before nodding in agreement, and that told her he was actually doing it—taking steps to be the man he was, and not the one he pretended to be.

But Brett was still nervous about meeting them, even more so after AJ had awkwardly asked her if she minded covering her tattoos.

Her first instinct had been *hell no*, but AJ had been honest about how traditional his folks were, and since his mother was already in poor health, Brett had decided it wouldn't be the end of the world if she pruded it up today. It was only for a couple hours, and besides, if her and AJ's relationship continued the way it was, his parents would eventually see her ink.

"Is this outfit okay?" she asked as she slid into the waiting Jeep by the curb.

Her distress grew when she noticed what AJ was wearing. Board shorts, T-shirt, and sneakers, an outfit that made perfect sense for a hot mid-June afternoon. Her attire, on the other hand, looked insane compared to his. Jeans to shield her legs, a cardigan to hide her arms, and socks to cover her feet, just in case she was asked to take off her shoes at the Walsh house. She would have to make a conscious effort to keep her sleeves from riding up; otherwise the ring of roses around her wrist would peek out.

"You couldn't find a lighter shirt than that?" AJ said skeptically. "You're going to be sweltering sitting by the pool."

She paled. "Pool?"

Oh God, what if his parents wanted her to go swimming?

"We won't be taking a swim," he assured her. "Honestly, I think it's just a show pool. I've never seen either one of my folks go in."

Brett fiddled with the edge of her sleeve. "I tried to cover everything up. That stuff you said about your mom being fragile after her heart attack freaked me out."

AJ sighed. "Shit. I'm sorry. I feel like an ass for even asking you to do it, but I just don't want to make any waves today. You should have seen the looks on their faces when they saw Reed's tats for the first time. They almost fainted in horror."

"It's okay. I'm not mad that you asked. I totally understand."

Did she, though?

She couldn't deny that she'd experienced a teeny-tiny pang of resentment when AJ had made the request last night. She wasn't used to altering her appearance to appease other people. She was *proud* of the way she looked.

A thought suddenly occurred to her. "That's another reason you don't have any tattoos, isn't it? Because they'd freak?"

He nodded, looking resigned.

"Well, I still think it's a damn shame. That hot bod of yours needs some ink." She batted her eyelashes. "And when you decide to get it, I know a great tattoo artist."

He snickered. "Not until I cash in on that bet, remember? You're the one who's getting another tattoo. Maybe a… hmmm…what are your thoughts on unicorns? Pink unicorns."

Brett gave him the finger. "Go ahead and keep threatening to choose something awful. We both know you won't follow through on it."

"You sure about that?"

She ignored his mocking smirk. "Oh, I'm sure. Because if you pick something mortifying, I'll strap you down to my chair and tattoo the words 'fuck you' on your ass. And I have experience with that, too—I did it for a client last month."

"Ha. I'm not letting you and your tattoo gun anywhere near me. Especially if you're in the same kind of mood you were in last night."

"She broke up with Damon!" Brett burst out, her disbelief over their TV marathon swiftly breaching the surface again. "How could I *not* be mad?"

Granted, yesterday's outburst might have been a *tad* excessive. But she refused to apologize for being passionate about her interests.

"Besides," she said accusingly. "You totally agreed with me. You know Elena belongs with Damon."

"Yeah…maybe…" AJ pursed his lips. "Sometimes I think she and Stefan might be soul mates, though."

"They are not. Damon is way more interesting."

"You girls just can't get enough of the bad boy, huh? Nice guys like me don't stand a chance."

"Ha," she mimicked. "You're not nice. Not after what *you* did last night."

A.k.a. shutting off the TV midepisode and taking her right there on the living room floor. Doggy style.

Nope, he wasn't nice. He was wicked.

Deliciously wicked.

"You enjoyed every second of it," he said smugly. His hand moved to the gearshift. "C'mon, let's get this show on the road."

Fifteen minutes later, he parked in front of a two-story home in a quiet neighborhood in lower Southie. The house was a lot more modest than Brett had expected, small and pleasant, with a lovingly tended garden and a white-picket fence, just as AJ had said.

She reached into the backseat to grab the dessert box she'd brought, then followed AJ to the bright green front door. He strode into the house without knocking, calling out a cheerful hello.

"We're out back," came a muffled male response.

From the pool, no doubt. Crap. Brett cursed the cardigan she'd worn, and mentally prepared for a couple of hours of being hot and sweaty.

AJ gave her a quick tour on their way to the rear of the house. They stopped in a spacious, cozy kitchen so Brett could put the pie in the fridge, then walked through the sliding door onto a large outdoor patio. The weathered deck led down to a small, kidney-shaped pool surrounded by another spectacular garden. There was a patio there as well, and Brett's pulse sped up as she spotted AJ's parents.

Blond hair like their son, but AJ had gotten his green eyes from his father. His mom's were deep brown, with thick eyelashes and faint wrinkles around the edges.

AJ wasted no time approaching his folks. He slapped hands with his dad, then hugged his mother before stepping back to introduce Brett.

"Hi," she said, feeling uncharacteristically shy as she shook hands with both of them. "It's so nice to meet you."

"Well, aren't you a tiny thing," Tom Walsh teased. He gripped her hand gently, as if he were afraid he might crush it.

And he probably could. The man was as tall and broad as his son, and far more muscular than she thought a windows and doors salesman would be.

"I'm tougher than I look," Brett answered, grinning as she gave his hand a firm shake.

AJ's mother was more guarded than her husband, her curious gaze sweeping up and down to assess the woman her son had brought home. Then the older woman's face relaxed, and she smiled widely, as if Brett had passed her unspoken test.

"I'm tougher than I look, too," Karen told her, then

hooked a thumb at her husband. "If only this one would quit coddling me. He's still keeping me from my garden."

Brett softened her tone. "AJ said you were ill a while back. I'm really sorry to hear that."

"Aw, thanks, sweetie. But I'm fine now." Karen tapped her left breast with gusto. "This heart of mine is stronger than ever. Come on, let's have a seat. AJ, pour Brett a glass of lemonade, will you?"

A moment later, Brett was seated next to AJ's mother, who was so sweet and bubbly that Brett couldn't help but like her. The four of them gathered at the table and chatted for a while. AJ's parents were intrigued when she told them she was an artist, but she left out the tattoo aspect of it and spoke instead about the black-and-white drawings she sold on the side. Eventually, AJ went inside to grab the apple pie Brett had brought, which delighted his mother, who thanked her profusely for the gesture.

So far, so good. Actually, things were going far better than Brett had anticipated.

She should've known her luck would run out.

"Lord, it's humid out today," Karen exclaimed, wiping beads of sweat off her forehead with the back of her hand. "Let's go dip our feet in the pool, sweetie. It'll be refreshing."

Brett tensed.

Crap.

Crappity-crap-crap-crap.

She glanced at AJ, whose face had gone expressionless. He didn't shake his head, didn't convey an unspoken warning, but she thought she spotted a muscle tic in his jaw.

She was helpless to argue, though. Karen was already dragging her toward the edge of the pool. The woman took off her sandals and dipped her toes into the crystal-clear water, sighing happily when her feet were submerged.

Brett remained standing, frantically trying to think of an

excuse.

And then…she stopped trying.

So what if Karen saw the little blue sparrows tattooed on her feet? She *loved* her sparrows. They made her happy. In fact, all her tattoos made her happy. Every line, every curve, every bit of shading and flash of color. She was an artist and her body was her canvas, and if Tom and Karen Walsh couldn't appreciate that, then to hell with them.

Because how was she ever supposed to convince AJ to be proud of himself if she didn't set an example?

Lifting her chin in defiance, Brett unlaced her shoes and peeled off her socks, then slid her cardigan off her shoulders and flopped down beside AJ's mother.

...

As Brett's arms were revealed, AJ swallowed a lump of dread, praying that his folks wouldn't comment. Or judge. Or do anything but continue to treat Brett with the same level of welcoming warmth they'd shown her this past hour.

But that was too much to hope for.

"Oh," his mother squeaked in surprise. She stared at Brett's angel as if she couldn't figure out what she was seeing. "Look at that."

A laugh rose in his throat, but he choked that down, too. His mother's eyes had traveled to Brett's dainty feet, which she was wiggling in the water, causing the sparrows to ripple as if they were about to take flight.

He glanced at his dad, whose startled gaze was also focused on Brett. When their eyes met, AJ offered a little shrug, but his father didn't look amused.

"I didn't realize you had tattoos," Karen said brightly, her cheerful tone betrayed by the tense set of her jaw.

"I have several," Brett answered with a smile. "A couple

on my legs, too."

That got her another "Oh."

Tom cleared his throat. "Did you, uh, draw them yourself?"

Brett twisted around to smile at him, too. "Some of them. My dad did the angel, and my older brother did the fish on my leg. They're both tattoo artists." A pause. "Like me."

"I see." His mother's mouth tightened.

AJ briefly closed his eyes. He hadn't asked Brett to lie about what she did for a living. He'd fully expected it to come out today. But he'd hoped his folks might pleasantly surprise him. Welcome Brett into the fold without a shred of judgment or disapproval.

Again, too much to hope for.

What followed was a lengthy discussion revolving around when Brett had gotten her ink done, why she'd done it, whether she planned on doing it again, and the best part, the sanitary implications of her using needles on her skin.

"Brett and her family take precautions to make sure everything is safe and that every piece of equipment is sterilized," AJ said brusquely. "Tattooing is a growing business, Mom. It's a respected profession."

His mother looked so unconvinced, and so revolted, that it triggered a wave of embarrassment. Brett's cheeks had turned bright red, her lips pressed together as if she were trying to bite her tongue. He didn't blame her. His mother was being a jerk, and he was so damn ashamed of her behavior.

He was about to force a change of subject when his mother did it for him. "I was meaning to ask you," she said, turning around to look at him. "Did Tamara get in touch with you?"

AJ froze.

So did Brett, before she swiveled her head too, her eyes voicing a silent question.

Tamara?

"We were chatting on the phone, and she mentioned you still hadn't called her." His mother's tone epitomized casual, but it was clear she wasn't oblivious to the rising tensions on the patio. "So I gave her your number. She said she sent you a message."

The look on Brett's face, a mixture of hurt and accusation, sliced into AJ's chest like a dull blade. Crap. Tamara *had* texted him. Last night, in fact, when he'd been in the process of making Brett come on her living room floor. He hadn't texted back, because, frankly, he didn't frickin' want to. But he had been wondering how on earth his old classmate had gotten his number.

Now he had his answer.

He looked at Brett, willing her to let it go, silently promising that he'd explain everything, but she lowered her gaze to her lap.

With that tiny act of rejection, AJ shot to his feet. "Sorry to cut this short, but Brett and I have to go," he announced. "I forgot we made plans with Gage and Skyler."

For once, the lie didn't burn his throat. He'd made up excuses his whole life, and each and every one of them had brought a sense of shame and self-loathing, but not today. If he didn't extricate Brett from this situation, she would inevitably lose her temper, and if that happened, he knew she'd regret it later.

Bullshit. You're leaving for your sake, not hers.

Hell. Did it matter whose sake it was for? Neither of them wanted to be here, damn it.

Brett practically leaped to her feet. "Right," she said in a shaky voice. "I totally forgot about that."

AJ stole a look at his father, who'd been sitting at the table in silence for the duration of the tattoo interrogation. Tom wore the strangest expression on his face, but for the life of him, AJ couldn't decipher it. He assumed his father was as appalled by Brett's "ghastly" appearance as his mother was, and AJ was pissed off at them both

As Brett hurriedly slipped into her socks and shoes, Karen stood up, too. "But you just got here," she said stiffly.

"I know, I'm sorry." AJ couldn't even muster up an apologetic smile. "But we have to go."

There were no hugs good-bye. No kisses. No assurances that he'd be back soon. He simply whisked Brett into the house, then out of the house, then into the Jeep.

He hadn't felt anger like this in years. His entire body trembled from it, his blood bubbled with it. His fingers were so stiff it was a miracle he managed to turn the key in the ignition. The temptation to storm back inside and force his folks to apologize to Brett was so overpowering that he fumbled for the gearshift, needing to get the hell away from the house before he did or said something he'd regret.

Before he could put the car in drive, Brett reached for the door handle. "I forgot my cardigan," she said flatly.

He reached for his own door. "I'll get it."

"No." The response was swift, hard. "I'll do it. You wait here."

AJ watched as she ran back to the house, her black hair whipping around her head like a storm cloud. Christ. She was pissed. So was he. He couldn't believe his mother had brought up Tamara like that. Merrily, deliberately, as if she'd wanted nothing more than to drive a wedge between him and Brett.

He wasn't going to let that stand. No way in hell. But he needed to take Brett home first. He needed to explain and apologize and get on his frickin' knees to beg her forgiveness.

Brett was gone for much longer than he liked, but just as AJ was about to go after her, the front door swung open and she reappeared. Her cheeks were flushed, and she had her cardigan draped over one arm.

She slid into the passenger seat without a word. AJ

stepped on the gas and drove away without sparing even a peek in the rearview mirror.

"Brett—" he started.

"Not now." She turned toward the window. "I just…I need a moment to think, okay?"

Frustration shot through him as she avoided his gaze. "I'm so sorry about that Tamara bullshit," he said softly. "My mom ran into her at the supermarket last month and decided to play matchmaker. I wasn't interested then, and I'm not interested now. I swear."

Brett shot him a sidelong glance. "Then why did you take her number?"

He faltered.

"You didn't use it, so your mother took matters into her own hands, but you *did* take it, didn't you?"

He let out a breath. Nodded.

Brett nodded in return. "Of course you did."

"I never, ever planned on calling her, Brett."

"I know that, too." A chord of sorrow clung to her voice. "You took the number to appease your parents. Because Tamara is exactly the type of woman they want you to marry and have kids with. We are talking about Ms. Perfect Cheerleader, right? Tamara from high school?"

He nodded again.

"Yeah, I can see why your mom is so eager for you to end up with her." Brett mumbled something AJ couldn't fully make out, but it sounded like "perfect."

After that, she went quiet again, and this time, when he tried to offer another apology, she simply shifted her eyes back to the passenger window. And there it was—the biting of her bottom lip, the groove in her forehead. She was deep in thought, and AJ sensed that he wasn't going to like it when she finally clued him in to her thoughts.

It wasn't until he pulled up in front of the Kims' general

store that Brett looked over again.

"AJ…"

Agony twisted in his heart. He knew what she was going to say.

"It's over."

Fuck. *Fuck.*

Knowing it and hearing it were two very different things. His heart was no longer clenching, but shattering. Splintering into pieces as those dark, beautiful eyes looked at him with such sadness and regret that his throat closed up.

"Don't say that," he said roughly. "At least let me apo—"

"Apologize?" she finished. "I don't need an apology, AJ. I'm not mad about the way your mom acted, or the fact that you got some other woman's number. Actually, I'm not mad at all."

She leaned in and touched his cheek, so gently it brought another painful squeeze to his chest.

"I can't be with you." Brett shook her head. "I tried to hide myself from your parents today by covering up my tattoos, but you've been hiding yourself from them for years. I've been watching you fight since I met you—not them, but yourself. You're trying so hard to be who you think you *should* be, instead of being who you are."

A denial rose in his throat, but it got stuck there.

"I saw you doing it with your friends, too." She sounded upset, frustrated. "You're trying to put on this good-guy image. Perfect son, perfect friend, perfect everything. You're trying to be Joey. But you're not him, AJ. You'll never be him."

Pain sliced into his chest. Her tone was so sad, so matter-of-fact. The urge to flee hit him hard, but he forced himself to stay put. He placed his fingers on the steering wheel, knuckles turning white as he gripped it tight, needing to steady himself with something. With anything.

"I know what it's like to lose someone you love," she

said quietly. "I lost my mother around the same age you lost your brother. But my mom would never have wanted me to be anyone other than myself. And I think Joey wouldn't have wanted that either."

Her eyes flashed suddenly, anger coloring her cheeks. "You *are* a good guy, AJ. You're sweet and compassionate and so frickin' good to the people you care about. But there's more to you than that. You run a successful business. You stick up for people even if you have to use your fists to do it. You like to fuck and fight and take chances. You get off on the adrenaline high from doing kinky shit in the bedroom, or punching some guy's lights out in a fighting match, and I *love* that about you."

AJ couldn't answer. Couldn't breathe. Every word she spoke was the truth, and it was making his head spin.

"It's not your fault that your brother died," Brett said, sounding tired now. "It was an accident. A very tragic accident. You were a little kid, and it *wasn't* your fault. But you've been trying to be a dead guy ever since." Her shoulders sagged. "And it's turned you into a ghost."

Panic skittered through him as she reached for the door handle. "Brett—"

"I can't be with a ghost. I want *you*, AJ—the real you, every part of you. I want him all the time, not just in private, but in front of the whole world, and until you can accept yourself for who you are, I can't be with you. I'm sorry."

Then she was gone. Out of the car and inside the building.

AJ stared at the empty space beside him, feeling as if someone had plunged a knife in his heart.

And that's when he realized he'd fallen in love with her.

Chapter Seventeen

"Can we talk?"

AJ looked up to see Darcy standing in the doorway of his office. He was supposed to be tending bar, but the thought of spending the night slinging drinks and chatting with faceless people was about as appealing as rolling around in mud.

Four days. It had been four days since he'd seen or spoken to Brett, and he was going through major withdrawal. He missed her with every fiber of his being. Couldn't go a single second without thinking about her. He'd almost called her hundreds of times since Sunday, but he'd stopped himself every time, because he wasn't sure what he would even say to her.

She'd been absolutely right. Every soft accusation, every resigned remark. But he was a fucking coward. He hadn't been able to stomach the idea of telling her how he felt about her, only to have her crush his heart all over again.

"AJ?"

Darcy waited expectantly—and nervously. He could see it in her blue eyes, in the way she wrung her hands together.

He gestured to one of the visitors' chairs. "What's up, Darce?"

Her reddish-blond hair spilled over one shoulder as she settled in the chair and crossed her ankles together. "Reed told me you and Brett broke up," she said tentatively.

"Yup." He couldn't control his bitterness. "Did you come here to gloat?"

Shame flooded her expression. "I guess I deserve that."

AJ didn't answer.

"I'm sorry." Darcy blurted out the apology, her entire face going pink. "I've wanted to say that to you for days, but I was too much of a wimp, and I knew that the moment I said it, I would have to admit why I acted like a jerk in the first place, and it was too frickin' embarrassing, okay?"

Curiosity penetrated the cloud of gloom he'd been battling since Brett had dumped him. He slanted his head, waiting for her to elaborate.

"I was jealous." Sheer misery darkened her eyes. "There. I said it. I was jealous."

His lips twitched.

"Don't you dare laugh at me," his ex-girlfriend grumbled. "This is mortifying enough as it is, okay? But Reed told me I had to man up and explain myself, so here goes. I took one look at Brett and I wanted to claw her eyes out."

AJ's brows soared to his hairline. Darcy was one of the sweetest, most laid-back people he'd ever known. Hearing her admit to experiencing violent urges was on par with finding out Mother Teresa was into BDSM.

"We were together for five months, AJ. Five months, and not once did you look at me the way you were looking at Brett."

Discomfort rolled in his gut. "That's not true."

"Yes, it is. And I'm fine with it now. I love Reed. I'm *happy* with Reed. But when I saw you and Brett together, I felt…I don't know, like I was lacking or something. I always knew there was something wrong with our relationship—you knew it too—but I figured it was both our faults. No chemistry or passion or whatever you want to call it." Darcy sighed. "But it was so obvious you felt passion for Brett. Like, an obscene amount of passion."

His stomach continued to churn, this time with white-hot regret that spiraled upward and tightened his throat. He'd felt passion, all right. Passion and excitement and *love*, damn it. He still did.

"So I started wondering if maybe *I* was the reason we didn't work out," she confessed. "And then I got mad and self-conscious and embarrassed, and I took it out on Brett. I'm so sorry, AJ. I really am. It was a dick move."

A laugh managed to escape his aching throat. "You were pretty damn rude," he agreed.

"I know," she wailed. "And I feel horrible about it. I finally got the nerve to ask Reed to bug you for Brett's number so I could apologize to her personally, but then he told me you two had broken up." She hesitated. "Why did you end it? Any idiot could see you guys were crazy about each other."

AJ swallowed. "I messed up."

It was all he said, and all he was willing to say. He was genuinely touched that Darcy had come to apologize, but he wasn't ready to tell her why Brett had broken things off. Any explanation he'd give required a shit ton of history he wasn't interested in sharing, not even with Darcy, who was one of the greatest listeners he'd ever met.

"Then fix it," she said bluntly.

He gnawed on the inside of his cheek. "That's easier said than done."

"Love is never easy, AJ. You have to work for it, fight for it. If you don't, then it'll just slip away, and you'll be left feeling miserable and alone."

Yup. Miserable and alone was precisely what he'd been feeling since Brett had walked out of his life.

Darcy approached the desk, bending down to plant a light kiss on his forehead. "I love you, you know. You're the best man I've ever known, AJ, and I want you to be happy."

"I know." He swallowed again. "I love you, too, Darce."

A knock on the half-open door sent both their heads swiveling toward it.

And talk about another surprise—AJ's parents were standing in the doorway.

His jaw fell open when he spotted them. His folks had never visited him at the club before. Hadn't stepped foot in Sin since AJ and his friends had bought it, and before today, showed zero interest in doing so.

"What are you guys doing here?" he demanded, unable to mask his shock.

Or his anger. Nope, couldn't hide that, either. He hadn't spoken to them since Sunday afternoon, despite his mother's numerous phone calls and text messages. In the end, he'd shot off a curt text saying he wasn't ready to talk, but he'd let her know when that changed, and he hadn't heard from her since.

As his parents took a hesitant step inside, AJ was wholly aware of Darcy standing at his side. He suddenly wondered if his folks had overheard the tail end of the conversation, the I-love-yous that had been exchanged, the tender kiss to his forehead.

If they had, they didn't comment on it, and AJ noted in bewilderment that his mother didn't greet Darcy with the same overjoyed expression she'd worn in the past.

"Darcy." Her tone was oddly reserved. "You look wonderful, sweetie."

"So do you." With a genuine smile, Darcy walked over to hug both his parents. "You look so much better from the last time I saw you," she told AJ's mother. "Are you feeling okay?"

"I feel great." Karen's gaze strayed to her son. "Physically, anyway."

AJ's dad cleared his throat. "Would you mind giving us a moment alone with Adam?" he asked Darcy.

"No problem." She squeezed Karen's arm before heading for the door. "We'll catch up another time."

The moment Darcy was gone, AJ warily got to his feet and looked at his parents, waiting for them to speak.

"Darcy looks happy," his mother remarked.

"She is." His tone hardened. "She and Reed are good for each other."

"It shows," she said with a nod. "I suppose we should have them over for dinner the next time you and Brett come by."

He let out a humorless laugh. "I don't think that's going to happen any time soon, Mom. Brett dumped me."

Lines of concern formed around her mouth. "Oh. Oh, no. Why would she do that?"

Disbelief spiraled through him. "Why the hell do you think?"

For once, neither one of them berated him for his language. If anything, they looked even more upset. Tom wrapped a protective arm around his wife's shoulders as she trembled with visible unhappiness.

When neither of them spoke, it triggered a rush of resentment. But what had he been expecting, an *apology*? Yeah, right. They'd probably throw a parade celebrating his breakup when they got home.

"I'm not perfect," he burst out.

They both blinked in alarm. "AJ," his mother started.

"No, I don't want to hear it, Mom. I want *you* to hear something. Both of you." His hands balled into fists as years of unvoiced anger breached the surface. "I can't be the perfect son you want me to be, okay? I've been trying to please you guys for years, because of..." His throat squeezed. He couldn't seem to say Joey's name out loud, so he hurried on in a shaky voice. "I've tried to be what you wanted me to be, but I can't do it anymore. I own a nightclub and I *like* it. I used to fight in a cage, and I *liked* it. You want me to be nice and polite and responsible, but sometimes I'm not, okay? And I'm tired of pretending to be."

"AJ—" his mom said again.

"I've been trying to be *him*, but I'm not, damn it! I'm *me*, and if you guys can't accept me for who I am, then..."

He trailed off, because really, how was he supposed to finish that sentence? *Then screw you?*

Silence crashed over the office, and then his mother murmured a question he hadn't expected.

"Did she break up with you because of us?"

His mouth fell open. *Seriously?* He'd just spilled his guts and *that* was the pressing issue on her mind?

AJ just stared at her

"Oh gosh. I'm so ashamed." Her entire body shook with distress.

Despite the anger and resentment clogging his throat, his protective instincts reared up. "Sit down," he said gruffly, rounding the desk to take her other arm. "You're supposed to be resting, remember?"

She allowed him to lead her to the visitor's chair, but the distraught expression didn't leave her face. "I didn't think...I didn't expect Brett to do that. Not after everything she..."

His eyes narrowed. "What are you talking about?"

His father sank into the other chair, and for a moment, AJ felt like the parent in the room. Looming over the older couple as they fidgeted in their chairs, avoiding his hawk-like gaze.

"What did Brett do?" he demanded.

His parents exchanged a look.

"Tell me, damn it."

"Language," Tom scolded, not letting him get away with cursing a second time. "And your mother is referring to the talking-to we got from your girlfriend on Sunday."

He blinked in confusion. Brett had barely uttered a word before they'd left the house. AJ had swept her away from his folks too quickly for her to give anyone a "talking-to."

Except...

She'd gone back inside to get her sweater.

Shit.

"What did she say to you?" he asked in a low voice.

His mother sighed. "What we needed to hear."

A brief silence hung over the room, until AJ's father spoke in a hoarse voice. "We don't blame you for what happened to Joseph. We never did."

The shock nearly knocked AJ off his feet. He had to grab the edge of the desk to steady his flailing equilibrium, but staying upright was a challenge when his lungs had stopped working. He blinked through the dizziness, unable to fathom what he'd just heard.

"Brett..." His voice cracked. "She told you...that I thought..." He couldn't finish. Didn't bother trying.

"She told us that you blame *yourself*," his mother said softly. "And the fact that you do...well, that just means we didn't do a good enough job telling you otherwise." Unshed tears clung to her eyelashes. "But your father's right, sweetie. We don't blame you. Joseph's accident...that's what it was. An *accident*."

AJ's teeth dug into his bottom lip, the guilt moving freely through his body and making his hands shake. "He wouldn't have been in those woods if it wasn't for me."

His mom was on her feet in an instant, her arms around AJ's neck as she held him tight. "It wasn't your fault," she whispered fiercely. "You were a little boy, and you ran away from home, just like millions of other little boys do. Accidents happen. Tragedy happens. It happens every day to hundreds of people, and it's awful and gut-wrenching, but people survive it. Our family survived it."

She released him, tears staining her cheeks. "And what you said just now... You're right about everything, sweetie. We *don't* know who you are." A pause. "We never even tried to find out."

"We've been acting like assholes," his father agreed.

His stunned gaze flew to his dad. He'd never heard his father curse before. Ever.

"We had an idea of who you should be, and we forced you to conform to it," Karen said sadly. "Whenever you made a decision we wouldn't have made ourselves, we offered nothing but judgment and criticism, and that wasn't fair to you, Adam. You have every right to be angry with us."

His throat burned. "I'm not angry with you."

"Yes, you are." Tom stood up with a shrug. "But that's okay. We're willing to work hard for your forgiveness."

"And we're dying to get to know our son," Karen said firmly.

His dad nodded in agreement. "Starting now. If you'd do us the honor, we would love a tour of this nightclub of yours."

AJ's heart expanded like a balloon as he stared at their earnest faces. Christ. They meant every word. The sincerity was in their eyes, their voices, their postures. And for the first time in his life, he got the feeling his parents were looking at him—and actually *seeing* him.

But as incredibly thrilling as that was, he knew he was about to let them down again.

"I'd love to—but it'll have to be another night. Right now I have to find someone and grovel for forgiveness."

To his surprise, his parents smiled.

"Groveling can be very rewarding," his father said

helpfully, the corners of his mouth crinkling with amusement. "Just ask your mom. God knows she's made me grovel hundreds of times over the years."

"It's true," she confirmed. "And your father happens to grovel very well." She paused in thought. "Maybe Reed and Darcy can give us the tour instead. Reed *is* around here somewhere, right? I haven't seen that boy in years."

Wonders never ceased—because it was the first time he'd ever heard his mother say Reed's name without following it up with a disparaging remark.

Well…shit. Maybe they really *were* willing to make a change.

"Sure, let's go track him down, and then I'll head out." He took a step to the door, then stopped to shoot his dad a mischievous smile. "Hey, Dad? Just a heads-up…I've never liked football all that much."

The older man growled. "Oh, hell no, Adam. That's just blasphemy."

AJ shrugged and grinned.

"No matter. You'll just have to pop by every Sunday come September and I'm sure we can twist your arm into liking it."

He cocked a defiant brow. "And if I don't?"

His father offered a shrug and grin of his own. "Then we'll just watch baseball instead."

Chapter Eighteen

She missed being AJ Walsh's girlfriend.

She really, really, *really* missed it.

So much that Brett still couldn't believe *she* was the one who'd ended it. But no matter how miserable she'd been these past four days, she wouldn't allow herself to cave. She'd meant every word she'd said—she couldn't be with him until he accepted who he was. No, until he *embraced* it.

Because if he didn't, he'd just keep living his life as two people. The man he was with her, wild and free and *wonderful*, and the man who struggled to follow in a dead boy's footsteps.

"Hey, princess, I'm taking off now."

She lifted her head at the sound of her father's voice. "Now?" she echoed, puzzled.

The grand opening of Conlon Ink North was three days away, and she and her dad had been slaving away to get the new studio ready for the public. Construction had finished, staff had been hired, ads had been booked, and word of mouth had spread. The shop was clean and sparkly and almost ready to open its doors, but Brett refused to let a single client walk into her tattoo parlor until every t had been crossed and every i had been dotted. Her brothers had teased her about being a perfectionist, but she couldn't help it. She was in charge now, and she wouldn't allow a single snag or hiccup.

"I thought we were supposed to go through the flash binders and take out all the outdated designs," she said accusingly.

"We'll do it tomorrow morning." Shrugging, her father ran a hand through his unruly beard. "I'll lock up when I leave so no one bothers you during the interview."

"What interview?"

"Oh, didn't I tell you? We've got one more applicant to see. He's waiting in the lobby. I'll send him in before I go."

There was someone else in the shop with them? Jeez, she really *was* out of it. For the past hour she'd been in the back pouring over stacks and stacks of flash—premade custom designs—and she hadn't even heard the front bell go off.

"Wait—what am I interviewing him for?" she exclaimed as her father made for the door.

"You'll figure it out."

The cryptic response only freaked her out more. So far, her father had sat in on every interview she'd conducted, and now he wanted her to do a solo one?

You'll be fine.

She clung to the reassuring voice in her head. She was worrying for no reason. Artist or piercer—those were the only two positions Conlon Ink had to offer, and she was perfectly capable of judging a candidate for either one. Except...she'd thought they'd already hired all the staff. Her father hadn't said a word about needing more help.

As footsteps sounded from the hall, Brett quickly straightened up the mountain of papers on her desk. God, she was *so* not prepared for this. Her office was a mess. Her tank top was inappropriately skimpy. This applicant was definitely not going to take her seriously.

"Come in," she called when a knock rapped on the door.

A second later, Brett stood up to greet her candidate—and gasped.

"Evenin', angel," AJ drawled. "You ready to do this thing?"

It took a second to unhinge her jaw from the floor. Then another one to properly steel herself against the incredible picture he made. Black pants, black T-shirt, black boots—the dangerously sexy attire told her he must have come from the club.

Dragging a hand through his short blond hair, AJ sat in the visitor's chair and looked around. "Nice office. Are you going to be spending most of your time in here, or at your tattoo station?"

Brett gaped at him. Had he seriously just waltzed into her office after four days of radio silence and started making small talk?

"What are you doing here?" she stammered.

"Interviewing for a position." An impish smile lifted his lips. "The position of Brett Conlon's boyfriend."

Her jaw fell open again and her knees got so embarrassingly shaky that she sank into her chair with an ungraceful *thud*.

"This is insane," she muttered, her brain still trying to process not only AJ's unexpected presence, but his even more unexpected announcement.

"More like unprofessional," he chided. "Do you tell all your potential employees that they're insane? That's not what you should be leading with in an interview, angel."

She just stared at him. His cheerful demeanor was starting to annoy her.

"Ask me why I want the job," AJ prodded.

Brett mumbled a curse under her breath, then decided

to humor him. He'd come all the way here for this craziness. Might as well let it play out.

"Fine. Why do you want this job?"

He leaned back in his chair, long legs stretched out in front of him as if he had all the time in the world. "Well, first off, I think I'd make an excellent boyfriend. I'll open doors for you and buy you flowers on your birthday."

She raised one eyebrow. "Very unoriginal. I can get that from anyone."

"I'll watch any teen vampire show you become obsessed with."

"Better, but not by much."

"Okay, how's this? I'll have sex with you whenever you want, however you want it."

A laugh struggled to break free. "Sounds intriguing. But still not a good enough reason for me to hire you. I have very high standards, Mr. Walsh."

"Trust me, I know." He looked like he was fighting a laugh too. "*Ms. Conlon.*"

"Then what else have you got?" she challenged.

Without breaking eye contact, he gripped the hem of his shirt and began dragging the cotton up his chest.

Brett's mouth went dry when his tight six-pack was revealed. "Don't you dare distract me with your bare chest," she ordered.

"Can't help it. I've got something to show you." He drew the fabric higher and exposed his pecs.

Brett gasped in shock. "Oh my God. What did you do?"

Heart pounding, she draped half her body across the desk to examine the small line of black text tattooed above his left pec.

It was a date.

Fucking hell—the idiot had gotten the day they'd met tattooed on his chest.

"Oh God, I really hope that's not permanent." But she knew it was. She could see it in the swollen redness of his skin, which told her the ink was only a few hours old. And she'd recognize that distinct style anywhere—this was Rob's handiwork, no doubt about it.

"Are you nuts? You finally get inked and *this* is what you choose?" she blurted out. "*The day we met*? What if we break up again, huh? Then you'll be stuck with the memory of me *forever!*"

AJ's laughter echoed in the office. "It's not just the day we met."

"Yes, it is!"

"Yep, but it's also the day I finally stopped pretending."

That shut her up. Hard. Her pulse sped up as she glimpsed the intensity in his eyes.

"That was the night I truly let go," he said quietly. "I gave in to the urges I was always fighting, and I did what I wanted. I *took* what I wanted. Even if you and I don't have a future—which we do, FYI—that night was important enough that I never want to forget it."

She was too stunned to move, let alone talk.

"So, you wanted to know what else I've got—this. A promise that I won't hide any part of myself, not anymore." His voice went husky. "From this point on, you get me. Just me."

Brett's heart skipped a beat as she studied his face. God, she'd never seen him look so...free. Was that the right word? Maybe *unburdened* was more apt. Relaxed. Open. Honest. Whatever adjective she used, they all reflected the same damn thing—something had shifted inside him, and it was written right there in his gorgeous green eyes.

"With that said...I like to fuck and fight and take chances," AJ said roughly, repeating the same words she'd thrown his way when they'd last spoken. When she'd broken up with him.

"Is that so?" she murmured.

He nodded. "But you know what else I like? Actually, you know what I *love*?"

"What?"

"You," he said simply.

Her breath jammed in her lungs.

"I love you, Brett. I love every second I spend with you." Conviction rang in his voice. "I like who I am when I'm with you, and I think you like who you are when you're with me."

He had her there. Being with AJ had taught her things about herself she'd never expected to learn. Like the fact that she *could* be in a healthy relationship. That she didn't have to be consumed by a man, that she could have fun without getting wasted and dancing on bar counters. That proving yourself was all the more rewarding when you had someone cheering from the sidelines, someone who was proud of you, someone who believed in you.

AJ was kneeling in front of her now, his warm hands cupping her cheeks. "Give me another chance, Brett. Let me be the man I know I can be."

"The man you are," she corrected.

"The man I am," he echoed. His thumb swept over her bottom lip in a tentative caress. "What do you say?"

She supposed she could have left him hanging. God knew it was always fun tormenting this man.

But her heart was so full of emotion it was dangerously close to overflowing, and the past four days without him had been too agonizing to ever have to endure again.

"You've got the job."

The boyish grin she loved so much made an appearance. "Yeah?"

"Of course." She rolled her eyes. "I love you, too, idiot. Did you really think I'd say no to that heartfelt speech?"

"The thought occurred to me," he admitted.

"Then you're an even bigger idiot." Laughing, she threw her arms around his neck and pulled him close. "Now kiss me before I change my mind."

As AJ's lips covered hers, a wave of sheer belonging washed over her. Oh yes, they belonged together, all right. They *fit*. Not just their mouths and tongues and bodies, but their *hearts*. She and AJ brought out the best in each other, and as long as he was willing to stop hiding who he truly was, then she was willing to open her heart to him.

They were panting when they pulled apart, foreheads resting together, AJ's hands gently stroking her hips.

"Makeup sex?" he suggested with a grin.

She grinned back. "Hells yeah." As his eager hands immediately tugged on her shirt, she quickly spoke again. "Oh, by the way, you should know, I—"

"*Son of a bitch.*"

His hiss of pleasure cut her off, and she knew he'd glimpsed what she'd been about to reveal.

Brett shivered as his features stretched taut with arousal, as his fingers skimmed up her rib cage so he could toy with the silver hoops on each of her nipples.

"When did you do this?" He growled out the question as he touched the nipple rings.

"The day after I broke up with you." She gave a sheepish shrug. "I do crazy things, too, when I'm upset. You should know that for future purposes."

He gave the piercings a little tug, sending a shiver racing up her spine. "Crazy? Nuh-uh, baby. This is the hottest thing I've ever seen." He licked his lips. "Can I put my mouth on you?"

She reluctantly shook her head. "Not yet. They're still healing."

"God." He growled. "You mean I'm going to be inside you, looking at these sexy fucking things, and I can't lick them?"

"Nope."

"Suck them?"

"Nope."

He cursed loudly.

Brett laughed and ran a reassuring hand over the five-o'clock shadow rising on his jaw. "You can lick and suck other things, if you want."

"Damn right I will."

His hands were already reaching for her waistband, and even though Brett's father had locked up, she still shot a wary glance at the open door, wondering if this was a good idea. This was her shop now. She had to set a good example for the rest of the staff.

Right?

Sensing her uncertainty, AJ chuckled and slipped one talented hand inside her jeans. "Come on, bad girl," he taunted, green eyes gleaming. "Are you gonna come out and play?"

Her reluctance melted away, replaced by a rush of reckless passion. "For you?" She leaned forward and grasped his zipper. "Always."

Epilogue

Three Months Later

"Did you ever in a million years think you'd see that?"

Brett jumped as AJ sidled up to her, his astonished gaze focused on the same astonishing sight she'd been gawking at. "Never in a trillion years," she corrected. "No, a *gazillion*."

On the other side of the small church, Tom Walsh continued to roar with laughter as Jimmy Conlon told an animated story that involved a lot of hand gestures and several meaningful winks. Next to them, AJ's mother chuckled over something Brett's brother had whispered to her. Karen warmly squeezed Mike's tattooed forearm and leaned in to whisper something in return.

Their families liked each other.

Brett was still reeling from the shock, even though she'd witnessed exchanges like this often in the past three months. AJ hadn't been kidding when he'd said that his parents were determined to make amends. Not only had they apologized to Brett and promised to stop judging a book by its cover, they'd actually followed through on it. Brett had spent a lot of time with AJ's mother since then, and it wasn't long before her hurt and resentment toward the woman had faded away.

Sure, Karen was still old-fashioned about some things, but she was warm and loving, and once she'd taken the time to get to know Brett, she'd been nothing but wonderful to her. Whether they were working in the garden or having lunch by the pool, Brett genuinely enjoyed Karen's company. It was nice having a mother figure in her life again.

And girlfriends, too. Jeez—figure that one out. Brett glanced across the room at Darcy, who had her hand on Gage's shoulder and was murmuring something in his ear. Gage looked drop-dead gorgeous in his tux, but he was broadcasting his nerves to the entire room. Brett totally got it, though. She'd be nervous too if it was *her* wedding day.

Darcy caught Brett's eye and grinned, as if she were enjoying seeing a man as big and intense as Gage giving in to wedding-day jitters.

Brett grinned back, though a part of her still wondered how on earth she'd managed to become best friends with the woman. Darcy's apology had paved the way, and after that, she and Skyler had welcomed Brett into the group with open arms. And today, Brett was about to stand up at that altar as one of Skyler's bridesmaids. Tattoos and all—including the new one on the inside of her right wrist. AJ had finally called in the bet, and as a result, Brett officially had a date inked on her skin. A date that matched the one on AJ's chest.

"Gage is nervous," AJ remarked.

"Yeah." Brett smiled. "But he won't be once Skyler walks down the aisle."

"Neither of them likes being the center of attention. I'm surprised they decided to do this whole church-wedding thing."

"Sky couldn't say no to her stepfather," Brett said with

a sigh. "He was determined to pay for a big wedding and an even bigger reception."

AJ's gaze swept over the beautiful white orchids crammed into every inch of the church. "When we get married, let's avoid all the fanfare. It kinda scares me."

"*When* we get married?" she teased, reaching up to tweak his bow tie. "Are you that confident I'd say yes if you proposed?"

"Yup."

"Yeah, well, talk to me once I've got this manager thing figured out. I can only handle one role at a time. Manager first. Wife? Maybe later."

"There's no maybe about it." He dragged a seductive finger over the tattoo on her arm. "We both know you can't say no to me, angel."

Brett couldn't argue with that. The only words that left her mouth in AJ Walsh's presence were *yes, God yes,* and *more please.* With the occasional *Oh God, that's good* thrown into the mix.

And she knew that the second the wedding reception came to an end, AJ would once again be coaxing those passion-laced words from her lips.

Over and over again.

As a shiver of anticipation raced through her, Brett shoved the dirty thoughts from her head and took AJ's hand. Then she led him to the altar so they could watch his best friend get married.

About the Author

A USA Today bestselling author, Elle Kennedy grew up in the suburbs of Toronto, Ontario, and holds a BA in English from York University. From an early age, she knew she wanted to be a writer and actively began pursuing that dream when she was a teenager. She loves strong heroines and sexy alpha heroes, and just enough heat and danger to keep things interesting!

Elle loves to hear from her readers. Visit her website www.ellekennedy.com or sign up for her newsletter to receive updates about upcoming books and exclusive excerpts. You can also find her on Facebook or follow her on Twitter (@ElleKennedy).

Discover the After Hours series…

ONE NIGHT OF SIN

ONE NIGHT OF SCANDAL

If you love sexy romance, one-click these steamy Brazen releases…

NO PROMISES REQUIRED
a *Love Required* novel by Cari Quinn

Professional football player Bryan Townsend is recovering from an injury preparing to attend his sister's wedding when he encounters a very sexy blast from his past—the stunning maid of honor. Bryan has no clue that Jill St. John was a virgin looking to broaden her sexual repertoire without risking her heart. But with every encounter they share, Jill is falling hard for the man Bryan has become. And now he must make the biggest play of his career—choosing between his team…or the woman he's always wanted.

TEMPTING HER FAKE FIANCÉ
a *Going Hollywood* novel by Julie Particka

Journalist Stasia Grant is in Vegas for the biggest interview of her career…and grappling with a broken heart, her cheating ex-husband, and a serious need for revenge. Her salvation comes from the most unlikely place—charming and sexy action star Evan Stone. After spending his life playing superhero, Evan has a plan for delicious satisfaction: a fake, week-long engagement and some no-strings fun to show Stasia's ex just what he's missing. Together, they're about to pull off the performance of a lifetime…but will they fall for their own con?

No More Mr. Nice Guy
a novel by Amy Andrews

Newly single Josie Butler just made herself a Sexy To-Do list (featuring Bad Boys only). To her mortification, her best friend's gorgeous older brother Mack finds it… and laughs. But when Josie goes looking for some sexy fun, Mack's nice guy side turns all hot bad-assery, and suddenly she's pinned against an alley wall. Hottest. Sex. Ever. Now Josie has found the perfect guy to work through her list. And it's the perfect plan, as long as no one finds out…and no one falls in love.

Chasing Trouble
a *Chasing Love* novel by Joya Ryan

Kindergarten teacher Jenna Justice has lived her life by the book—right school, right career, right image. Too bad the townsfolk of Diamond, Kansas, have a hard time forgetting that she wasn't born on the right side of the tracks. Away from prying eyes, she allows herself one sizzling, fantasy-filled night with her best friend's bad boy brother, Colt McCade. His fast-and-loose reputation could cost her everything she's worked for, but walking away might cost him more…

Printed in Great Britain
by Amazon